To my Bestess fr
ever. You r a beautiful
person. I am so proud
of u. I ♥ u much.

MISTY HELMS

Eternal Life

Diary of an Immortal Soul
October, 1337–June, 1358

First Edition

PAGE PUBLISHING, INC.
New York, NY

First originally published by Page Publishing, Inc. 2014

ISBN 978-1-62838-715-5 (pbk)
ISBN 978-1-62838-716-2 (digital)
ISBN 978-1-62838-717-9 (hardcover)

Printed in the United States of America

To everyone who gave the inspiration and support that I needed to write this book: Thank you.

Special thanks to my husband and children for their love and patience.

Introduction

I have read a lot of different books, most of which I never finished. A lot of the writers seemed to get carried away with so much detail that I would get impatient with them getting back to the point of the story. Most of the drawn out things didn't seem important.

One day, I had expressed this to my husband and he made a good point when he said, "You know, a lot of readers love even the smallest detail. It makes things more vivid for the imagination. I bet if you wrote a long enough story, you would find yourself adding more detail for the imagination of the reader." After he said that, I decided that I would give it a try.

Tragic Life

I guess I'll start where it all really began for me. Anything before that was no more than just a memory to me. First let me give you an idea of the world I grew up in.

My name is Pandora Porchillo. My mother said that she gave me the name Pandora because when she opened the box to deliver me, hell followed.

I was born in a small cottage on the outskirts of Venice, Italy on October 13, 1337. The Dark Ages were still in full swing, and sometimes I think they still were. Chaos, death, war, plagues, poverty, and superstitions were at an all time high. Most of these superstitions have lingered in time for centuries.

Christians were raging such a war for power that even the Catholics were not safe from this. They hid their agenda by claiming to be doing God's work. If you ask me, Mr. Great n' Powerful almighty doesn't need anyone to do his job. That's what makes him God.

Sometimes it was so bad that wearing red or giving a pinch was enough to be accused of dealing with the devil and to be executed. Millions of women and thousands of men would be tortured and murdered in horrifying ways publicly to be made example of, instill fear, or not take responsibility for thyself. Many children were orphaned, like my mother, and some were also murdered because bible thumping tyrants—wealthy and poor alike—were forcing their religion upon the world, and most of the world took the bait. People stopped taking responsibility for the actions of their own freewill. They started blaming pagans, wiccans, black majick, demons, the devil—anyone and anything but themselves. It's called freewill. To say that the devil can overpower, it was like saying that he's more powerful than God 'cause not even God can do that.

Before the religious began their wars, it was not so frequent and didn't last anywhere near as long. As a matter of fact, there had not been a war after that had lasted even a fraction of that long. The religious wars lasted a near eight hundred years and created a death toll larger than the world had ever seen—ranging from 1–9 billion. It also brought out the worst in humanity. Racism, paranoia, harsh skepticism, and unreasonable fear, alongside with judgment reigned. It also paved the way for satanic cults and the resentment of God. One that was more misunderstood than any other god nowadays.

The Dark Ages had flooded over the entire world. With so much death in the air diseases of all kinds, most unexplainable to this day, swept across Europe, Asia, and Africa adding greatly to the death toll. No one was untouched by the immense amount of suffering the world had endured. Rich or poor strong or weak, no matter of race, everyone suffered one way or another. So yes, my memories of that life were full of more dark than light.

My mother was an Italian pagan whom, like I said, was orphaned as a child, and my father was Persian. During his travels through Africa, he became a shaman—harmless religions that the Vatican had been trying to abolish for over 150 years by the time I came along. All the things my parents had been were frowned on in more ways than one, so you could only imagine how hard life was for them. Their union was unheard of and forbidden to society. My father's religious beliefs and the scar that stretched down through his cheek from his patched-eye socket frightened most but not my mother; she only saw the good within.

They met when they came across one another during travel and fell in love instantly. My father was taken by my mother's beauty, and she was taken by the purely good soul she saw in him. Two years later, they were blessed with my brother Michael. For his safety, they kept traveling and hid their practices well bouncing around Europe. On March 7, Michael's seventh birthday, my mother and father found out that they were going to have another child.

Sadly, a month later, my father died. An old friend of his from somewhere in Asia visited for a night during his travels. He left early the next morning after mentioning that he was not feeling well. Within two weeks, a disease took my father. It was a new and rare disease until it left a horrifying mark on the world ten years later. My mother remarried a wealthy Celtic man to hopefully insure her security for us. They moved to Venice, and there, events occurred at the exact moment of my birth—thereafter the wrong light shined in my direction..

It just so happen that thirty years before the exact moment of my birth, the Knights Templar were murdered for being so-called traitors against God and the crown according to the king of France. Due to the horror of that day, thirteen was considered a very unlucky and evil number. To make things even worse the most horrific plague in history was right behind me, and it would come or go as it pleases for seventy-five years consuming three-fourths of Europe and Asia's entire population. It was all a perfect recipe for hate and fear from others.

The Beginning

As soon as I took my first breath, my stepfather put his hand over his heart and fell to the ground. As he fell, he knocked Michael, who was standing next to him, back into a table causing a knife to fall off the edge of and penetrate his little eight-year-old chest.

Doctor Tirracelli, the doctor who delivered me, put me in my mother's arms to tend to my stepfather. The doctor was too late. He was dead as soon as he hit the floor. Dr. Tirracelli then went directly to Michael's side. He tried to stop the bleeding and resuscitate Michael. After ten minutes of trying, the doctor declared him dead. Dr. Tirracelli was just about to scurry out the door to go get help with the bodies when my brother's eyes popped open as he deeply gasped for air.

My mother, who was trying to pull herself together in the middle of a nervous breakdown, gasped also in relief and reached her hand in

Michael's direction. She told him that she was there in hopes to comfort him. Dr. Tirracelli picked Michael up gently and held him while sitting in a chair then carefully examined him.

Dr. Tirracelli stitched Michael's wound, laid him in his bedroom, and came to talk to my mother. "I don't know how to explain it, but Michael will be well with good rest and medicine that I left by the bed. I am going to clean you up and awake my assistant to come help me remove your husband's body. I am truly sorry for your loss." He looked at my mother with sympathetic eyes laying his hand on her shoulder. My mother nodded with tears in her eyes still trying to hold on to her sanity.

Dr. Tirracelli walked out swiftly. My mother then looked down at me laying still and breathing lightly in her arms. Then she pondered at the fact that not once did I whimper or whine to be fed or comforted. Not even throughout all that had happened. I was fast asleep. Dr. Tirracellis assistant unfortunately was one who loved to gossip so the story spread and changed from person to person. Each person grew more and more suspicious of a single, non-Christian woman with two small strangely colored children one of whom came back from the dead, and the rumors got worse. We didn't live there long.

We moved around a lot, staying away from population as much as possible. Mother schooled my brother and I well on paganism, Wicca, shamanism, and other religions such as spell crafting, natural healing, and some defenses against dark arts and true evil.

Michael and I would help at farm for food and irrigate for water; Michael also taught me to hunt, so we didn't have to go into town. But no matter how many times or how far we moved, bad things would continue to happen. Like a curse was haunting my soul. Most of my friends had died, disappeared, or turned against me. When I was five, a family who were good friends to us died in a house fire; the cause was *unknown*. Al a couple of teenage boys who were friends with Michael died of natural causes. Back then dying so young was no more natural than it was today.

The world's population dwindled due to mysterious plagues; people were being killed in many ways for all kinds of reasons. The only luck we had was that we didn't catch so much as a cold and were able to avoid getting killed. Of course people grew suspicious and we would have to move again. Moving became not so often when our mother decided to keep us away from civilization. She would even reject people just passing by, for their own good. Michael and my mother would try to convince me that it was nothing. Bad things happened to people every day all around the world. My mother would say that you can't be in two places at once.

It became harder to believe as time went on. At only six years of age, I even stopped believing in coincidence. It became, to me, an illusion people used to make themselves feel comfortable and to explain the unexplained. The only thing that comforted me was my dreams. The dreams were all different scenarios but the same character; a gigantic black dragon that would dance and play with me. Sometimes he would soar so high with me on his back that it was like touching heaven. Heaven to me was being far away from the rest of the world.

When I was eight, we moved into a small house outside of a forest near Florence. The last place we lived. My brother and I used to sneak out every night. He would hold my hand guiding me to a path he discovered deep in the forest while exploring one day. It led to a beautiful clearing. The trees made almost a perfect circle, and the moon with the stars at its side lit up the clearing just brilliantly around eleven o'clock every night faithfully. The grass was as soft as silk and as plush as a feather pillow with little blue flowers that seemed to each be pointing at a star. The temperature would be quite warm at night, but in the clearing, a light cool breeze would come with the smell of grapes at a nearby large vineyard. The clearing was pretty big, so the moon would be our light in the sky for about three hours before it began to pass by and dim its silvery light.

Michael and I would talk or play hide-and-seek, or sometimes we would just lie in the cool grass and try to find as many shapes in the stars as we could. We would of course practice some of the things that mother had taught us every time we were there. It was a perfect place for meditation. Nature's energy heals the soul and calms the mind. Much needed after a hot day of farming and house work. One night though became the last night that I would see my brother for eight years.

June 25, 1347

Michael and my mother had seemed a little distant all day yesterday, and they said everything was okay when I asked, but I knew otherwise. My intuition had been screaming at me.

Last night, Michael snuck me out later than usual, and on our way to the clearing he was unusually quiet and slow paced. Procrastinating so he could think about how to say what it was that was so heavy on his mind. I was also quiet and wondering what was going on and trying to think of something that I could say to break the ice. When we got to the clearing, I stopped yanking my hand from his gentle grasp. "Michael Porchillo!" I said sternly. "What is troubling your mind so much so that you stay silent?" I asked, frustrated from the confusion.

Michael kept his back to me staring at the moon. Then he hung his head and took a deep breath struggling to get the words out. "Pan, I'm leaving." He turned to see me looking at him still confused.

"What do you mean leaving?" I said realizing that the sound of his voice didn't give me the feeling that he was going to be back any time soon.

Michael knelt down on one knee. "Momma had a premonition when she was seven-months pregnant with you, and she had been preparing me for it ever since. I am sorry that it was kept from you, but there is no way I can make you understand. Not yet. Horror is coming fast and when you turn eighteen, the worst will be at your doorstep. As much as I hate to admit it, I cannot protect you on my own. Momma is sending me for help and to find an elixir called eternal night. She could not, or maybe even did not want to, tell me much more than that." He put his hand on the side of my face. I looked at him trying to contain the panic and little bit of anger that was trying to punch through my chest. Tears began to make their way down my cheek like a steady creek.

"You can't…I mean…how can you just," I said sobbing. I paused for a second to flutter my eyes so that I could see his face. His black hair was pulled back but still shined under the moonlight and his bright green eyes were misty from trying to contain his own painful tears. "Take me with you," I said hopefully with a desperate look on my face.

"No, I can't," he said sternly. I took a step back away from him, and he stood up as a tear rolled down his soft cheek.

I could feel the pain and anger ripping through me like a tidal wave of daggers. "Why not? Did Momma tell you not to, or do you not want me to go with you?" I snapped while crossing my arms over my chest to keep it from exploding.

He creased his eyebrows and pursed his lips then spoke softly and said, "I want nothing more than to be able to take you with me and Momma said nothing of it. It is that you cannot come. I am doing this to save and protect you. If I take you with me in the dangers I will face, there is more of a chance of me loosing you. I could not live with that. Beside, you and I are all Momma has left. It will be hard enough for her with me gone. If I take you she has nothing to love and nothing to love her back." I dropped my arms and looked down to my side. The grass and blue flowers were blurred together like a washed out painting. He was right about Momma. I couldn't do that to her. I was not going to win this one.

I took a deep breath and exhaled jaggedly then I looked at Michael and he stepped toward me. All I could do was throw my arms around him, just above the waist, and hold on tightly as tears burst through my eyes. Michael got down on both knees and embraced my hold. I laid my head on his shoulder and tried to contain myself enough to speak. "How long will you be gone?" I asked in a winning soft tone,

"That I'm unsure of. I do promise though that I will be there when horror comes." Michael caressed my hair.

"When will you leave?" I pushed out sobbing.

Michael sighed. "Tonight. I have already said my farewell to Momma. This was discussed just this morning and my first stop is a day's travel." I squeezed him harder, crying as I nestled my head in the middle space of his neck and shoulder.

Michael pulled back and reached into his pocket. "I have something that I think you should have," he said as he pulled out a silver necklace, and hanging from it was an amethyst, raw and unpolished. Silver was woven around it holding it in place protectively. He placed it in the palm of my hand and closed my hand around it. I looked at him and he grinned. "For protection. One of the most powerful stones used for that purpose," he said. He then looked up to the moon, "Not long before the dawn now. I will take you home. From there I begin my journey." I took a deep breath and dried my eyes. He took my hand, and we began the slow walk back home.

I couldn't help but feel like a crack ruptured in my soul. My lungs seemed to struggle with breathing correctly, almost like someone had reached inside of me and held a tight grip on them, and my heart, oh my poor heart. Words could not describe the pain of my broken heart. Michael was not only my brother but my best friend—my only friend. When we got back home we tearfully said our good-byes, and I watched him ride off, disappearing into the darkness of the forest.

Today the pain was still strong and our hearts were heavy from missing Michael, but I know mamma needs me as much as I need her. It helps having the schooling, chores, and religious practices to steer my focus away from the sorrow. Unfortunately, with me finding more ways to occupy myself; I am sure that it will leave me with little time to write in my journal.

For example, tomorrow Momma and I were beginning to dig an escape tunnel. I must admit that I don't like living in a time that makes the tunnel necessary. With it being just the two of us, the tunnel will take a lot of dedicated time and effort. So I will say good night and pray for Michael's safety.

October 13, 1347

The tunnel was coming along nicely though we didn't work on it today. On my and Michael's birthday, Momma declared no work or chores for the day.

Momma had been doing her best to keep me company. We grew closer every day. Missing Michael gets easier to handle day by day though we have not heard a word from him yet. I trust Michael was alive and Momma knew. She can see things like that.

Today was my first birthday without Michael and it was different but a good day nonetheless. Momma spent the day preparing my favorite meal along with her amazing pecan pumpkin pie from scratch.

We sang and danced by the fire then we played a game that father had taught Momma and Michael called Moncala. Before we retired to our rooms, I listened to Momma telling me a beautiful story about a dragon that fell in love with a young girl.

The story made me wonder…when I become a woman, will a man ever love me the way father loved Momma or the way the dragon loved that girl? Will I ever find love or will that die too? I didn't tell Momma when I think like that. It makes her sad and with the things to come, the things that she prepared for the things that she fears…she's got enough on her shoulders.

Poor Momma, I do worry about her so much. She was left to raise a child on her own in a time when unreasonable fear of death or being forced into poverty and violence was rising to new heights every day. No man to cut the wood or help harvest the crops. If something needed to be fixed, Momma would fix it. In these crucial upcoming years in my life, I have heard her tell the gods in prayer that she is worried about me having no male figure in my life to look upon nor to fight off the wolves. She worries that she cannot do enough, but in my eyes, she does more than enough every day. I wish I could do more. Momma tells me that my smile is enough and I hope that stays true.

December 19, 1347

Word came that a relentless epidemic had begun to spread in Europe. It claimed twenty-three million in Asia and here many have already died. Momma said she feared us encountering this pestilence. I think that she feared the locals more than this plague though.

I don't know which was worse. Orthodox Christians and Catholics were no more innocent than the pestilence. They were just as ruthless and spread like wild fire with no mercy. They have and still do cause just as much pain and suffering. This plague seems to do it in less time though. Now those religions were using the pestilence to their advantage. They say it was God punishing people like my mother and I, and that our religions were to blame. In my opinion, the world was full of so much decaying death and unseemliness that there will continue to be undefined illness. No one was to blame but the ones who string bodies about to rot.

Momma does her best to keep my mind off of the daily tragedy by allowing me to help with preparation for the Winter Solstice.

Still there was no word from Michael. I worry that this deadly illness had reached him. But Momma had been reminding me that the journey he had taken was long and dangerous. Knowing that, it helps diminish the fear. It leaves room to think that he was alive and well just trying to stay hidden. Contacting us could lead something or someone to us, him, or both. With the pestilence becoming so strong in the air, I pray the gods would hear my plea for his safety.

Today, I helped Momma make wreaths and garland to decorate the house tomorrow and a few of her pagan friends made their yearly trip to our house. I call one of them auntie she's been Momma's truest friend since she was a child and thankfully they too still have their good health.

They only come once a year for the winter solstice celebration, but they bring their children and having children around like me, even if it was only once a year, it was a blessing. We get to play, dance, and laugh. We get to be children. Momma always hosted the best and most beautiful winter celebration. Everyone was looking forward to it!

I must go now. Streaming the ribbons was my favorite part and I wanted to help.

April 15, 1348

The pestilence had been given a name and I must say it fits all too well. It was now known around the world as the Black Death. Since I last wrote, Black Death had vastly spread its evil rampage into Florence. The most common signs were the gavocciolis (tumors) that form on the neck, the armpits, or groin area and eventually bleed with clear ooze mixed into the blood. Once the gavoccioli was spotted, a person's life expectancy was only a week, at the most. Death was ramped in the streets. The smell of towns and villages near and far burning their dead was absolutely nauseating. Hogs running loose on the streets of Italy's most prominent town were dropping dead from feasting on corpses that had been thrown out to make room for the still living. Flies and mosquitoes dinned on the bloody rags of the ill that have carelessly been discarded on the streets of Florence. The meek had no chance.

These horrifying displays and the risk of such a death was why Momma won't let me out much beyond our backyard. I missed the oak tree in the backyard. Its leaves were always so green and abundant. I did long to be able to sit at the bottom of the trunk and rest my back on it while reading a book or making a head piece out of wild flowers, but now it seemed that old faithful was dying. All the smoke from burning bodies had begun its strangling hold on all plant life by blotting out the suns nourishing rays. Playing out back, dancing, or whatever else I could think up was how I made the day go by, but when the air outside became deadly it was yet another thing I have to let go of. The Black Death took more than the life in your body.

June 18, 1348

People were still dropping in mass numbers. I feared that the Black Death would wipe out the world before it was gone. At night I can hear the cries of men, women, children who had lost loved ones, and my constant nightmares of seeing the poor and hungry dying on the streets was growing tiresome.

In those dreams I walk through the poverty-stricken streets of Paris, London, Sicily, small villages in Asia, and more. People lay quarantined outside of their homes dead or very close to it. Their bodies were scarred and pale, even sunk in. Mothers lying limp were holding their lifeless infants Orphans crying sitting next to their dead parents. Momma had been sleeping in a chair by my bed. My nightly cries worry her.

As I predicted, the extra work had kept me busy. Now we are on way to the Summer Solstice in which we travel to Rome to see Auntie. Rome was breathtaking this time of year. I admit I am excited although…I have not enjoyed the pungent smell of decayed and burning bodies that still dances in the air. I almost wonder if Rome will still behold its seductive beauty…nonetheless we will arrive in a day's time.

Momma and I are beginning to accept the fact that we might not ever hear word from Michael. It's most frustrating at times. I do wish he was with us.

Momma had been schooling me in depth and doing it well. I can move small objects with my mind and open locked doors without touching them. It's quite fascinating. My math skills are getting better too. Mamma said that there were still so much more work to do before my thirteenth birthday.

Momma doesn't believe that thirteen was such a bad number. She says that it's my good luck number—my power number. It's amazing how much math and science have to do with the supernatural as well as nature itself, as we see it. My thirteenth birthday was two and a half years away and yet Momma had already begun the planning for an in depth celebration. She calls it a path to womanhood celebration.

The tunnel was getting so close to being done. Momma and I have been anxiously working from dawn till late in the evening. This was almost like a vacation.

October 13, 1348

I have become used to the smell of death. In less than two years this demon pestilence had more than lived up to its name with poverty at its side. So far the number of diseased had already gone into the hundred thousands. Momma and I cloak ourselves at night and bring food to surviving orphans along with blankets and herbal medicine that Momma makes. It was horribly terrifying to see so much death and chaos. It's even scarier to know that anyone who's got so much as coughs or sneezes was quarantined on an island not too far from here. There was a hospital there, but even before the plague nothing but horror stories about the hospital and its resident doctor were told. The poor people sent there. They had already lost everything only to be faced with torture. When going to that island…if you're not plagued by this pestilence, you will be. The pleading cries for help and screams of pain; even from children; can be heard at night…it was haunting.

Seeing the thankful relieved smiles on the faces of the ones we help bring a sense of pride and slight comfort.

We finished the tunnel two months after my last entry just in time for the first harvest, which I must add I was surprised we had anything to harvest.

Amongst everything else, Momma also had me working harder and harder on my spell crafting as well as my general education. With their only being the two of us tending to the crops along with harvest time and caring for the animals, it was more time consuming.

I still find myself staring at the once abundant old oak tree. I day-dream about the retrieve from the sun's rays when sitting underneath it, and how the leaves shimmered in the sun when the sweet grape smelling breeze came by. This last summer, the air had been fatally unpredictable so I was unable to enjoy those same simple pleasures. Momma made some cloths out of hemp that cover our mouth and nose to filter the air we breathe in when we do our night time Good Samaritan bit. Lately we wear them while tending to the gardens outside, though we move quickly in hopes to not breathe in death before we go inside.

During the fall season, after a day in the garden, Momma and I sit by the fire to talk, read, draw, and practice the less-complicated spell casting. Momma loves to show me some of the things she can do. Things I won't be old enough to learn till I turn eighteen.

I decided that I would write in my journal at least once a year and I couldn't think of a better time than my birthday. After all it was the only day that I have for myself.

October 13, 1349

This past year had been harsh for Momma and me. Still there had been no word from Michael; Black Death's toll had soared to the millions, and in early December of last year, Auntie was abducted by a Christian mob and murdered. She was on her way to us for the Winter Solstice. To make things worse, the only local friends of no religious preference that we knew were forced to flee from their own home buy the local priest and a few faithful followers. Then during a Pagan

Summer Solstice ritual this year, on the outskirts of Paris, the king of France ordered an attack on us. It was terrifying hearing the pleading screams of women and children as we scarcely made our way to safety with only a few others.

All pagan and Wiccan alike have had to result to hiding our rituals and practices deep into the darkest forests. I guess Sherwood Forest was still rumored to be haunted...ha-ha!

Momma had begun to practice get away plans with me. I almost fear turning eighteen, and I can barely remember the last time I saw the sun. Its bountiful rays have long been blocked by grey clouds of smoke from the fires of the burning dead spreading throughout Europe. The fires that were not caused by war or terrorism were set to eliminate ones that died of the Black Death. Some of the bodies are burned along with everything they possessed or touched and some are just simply disposed of. In Paris the dead are stacked in underground tunnels.

We celebrated my birthday nonetheless, and Momma did an amazing job at making sure it was better than the last as she always had. Momma made me a beautiful charm bracelet with jewels of all kinds along with tiny silver stars and pagan symbols. I can't wait till my thirteenth, Momma said she's gonna have something even more special for me.

Well the night was going by quickly, and I am getting tired so goodnight and farewell till next year.

October 13, 1350

These times are tumultuous. Horse-bound invaders have been charging countryside, and religious conflicts are getting worse. Muslims have conquered many lands. The scarcity of sound literature and cultural achievement scares me while barbarous practices prevail.

I do wonder from time to time if there are any of us left and even more so I am beginning to wonder if Michael was ever coming back. Momma no longer knew and I struggle to keep the hope alive. Black Death had consumed over fifty million lives and was still hungry for more. That's not counting the victims of other diseases that have evolved in this plague's steps. These diseases were said to be easier to fight off and the symptoms were less severe but they moved too quickly.

With everything combined, the world was a mess. The water was still unclean and the sun's rays still struggle to find its way through. Some crops and vineyards have died and some farm animals were getting sick too. People were losing their livelihood and growing bitter. They had been turning to the churches and not a single free-thinking woman in the world was safe. I hope the locals have forgotten that we even exist. I haven't seen another human being in over a year.

My thirteenth birthday was as good as Momma promised. Momma's gift was breathtaking. It's a raw emerald as big as the palm of my hand. She had put it in my hand then closed my hand around it and said, "Keep it close, my love. It will guide and protect you." I was honored but even more excited. I'm still holding it now as I sit here writing and the excitement had drained me. I am tired. Good night to thee till next time.

October 13, 1351

Another year had come and gone and I missed Michael so much. Momma had tried to accompany me as much as possible; still she knows that sometimes it's just not the same. Just two months ago, Momma and I cried together. The thought of never seeing him again had crossed both of our minds not to mention, I am becoming more convinced that Black Death was determined to exterminate mankind before it goes away.

On a good note, my energy was getting stronger and yet Momma limits me. There's something she's hiding, but I do believe it's for the best. The strength of my energy had given me a bit more confidence.

It's sad to say that the town had become almost ghostly. If anyone was left when this was over, rebuilding and bringing back sanity will take quite some time. Harsh religious campaigns are still sweeping across Europe and growing fast around Italy. I thank the gods for every year I still get to write about the life I lived during such times.

I have been having more frequent nightmares about small fights, big battles, and the newest one I had last night was more like hell. I was fighting in a great war…an unimaginable great war. Momma didn't always know how to explain them, but she always had a way of comforting me.

October 13, 1352

The Black Death had miraculously begun to retreat, and I saw a ray of sunshine make its way through the smoky air. It shined bright on the old oak and for a moment worth remembering I saw hope, which I needed.

Momma had been getting nervous and this year was different. I had almost begun to feel like a prisoner of the house. It seems as though Momma fears for my life more and more every day. She had covered the windows, and I helped her build a tall fence around the back. The only sunlight I get was in the backyard. I have no friends, and yet I don't want any. Not too many worth trusting. I stay optimistic and hold onto the hope that if Michael was dead then he's watching over us.

Something new and concerning had risen inside my mind when I sleep. Every night for the past three months, I awake in a cold sweat then, I hear someone faintly say my name. When I go to the window to see who it might be…I don't see anything but the moonlight illuminating the backyard until a shadow big enough to blot out the night sky flickers by three times. The shadow brings violent gusts of wind when it comes and takes it away when it leaves. I haven't said anything to Momma yet not sure what to think of it myself. It seems impossible for it to be just a reoccurring dream. I will say this though…if another three months go by and it still comes…I will have no choice but to tell her.

We still celebrated my birthday and it was good. Momma made a cake that was just amazing and gave me a hand woven blanket. The blanket was died with berry juices to create a burgundy color. She also stitched Celtic trinity knots on it with black thread. We danced, sang and laughed.

Now was when I say good night and hope that the gods allow me to live on another year.

October 13, 1355

Over the past three years, Momma had pushed me harder than ever—with everything. My last two birthdays were still celebrated but with exhaustion. So writing was not heavy on my mind. This birthday, my eighteenth was different. Her smile was not so reassuring anymore, her worry grew every second that went by, and she hadn't stopped cooking since she got up. She still won't tell me why she was pushing me so much on my practices. Though she pushed so much; she also never failed to show me love and compassion.

Italy was still trying to crawl out of the darkness that once consumed it. Other deadly diseases still linger, but the biggest problem was the country's recovery and last but not least, I am sorry, this might be my last and shortest entry.

As Florence began the struggle to recover itself, the town's people would become suspicious of my mother and me remaining unaffected and untouched by everything. Our crops flourished while others died. Our pigs, horse, sheep, and cows always grew healthy when others would not. Finally, suspicion turned into fear and impatience. So two days after my eighteenth birthday the people of Florence decided to take action.

The day started off like any other day for us. Though tension was unusually high and abundant in the air; Mom had been busy the last couple days making more food than we needed. When she was done she packed it up as if getting ready for a long trip then she would hide it in a secret storage hole at the end of the tunnel which was hidden in the small stables outback. I knew that something was coming, something was very wrong and my anxiety grew with every second that went by.

Late in the afternoon my mother went to store away the little bit of food that was left and I was straightening the house when I heard a commotion in the distance.

My mother burst through the door and I quickly turned around startled. There was panic written all over her face. She latched the back door came to me then gently put both hands on each side of my face brushing some hair away. "It's time, my love," she said softly. My heart dropped. I knew that she would not be coming with me. Tears began to fill my eyes, "Oh, now don't cry. I will always be with you." She was trying to comfort me and it worked only a little, but the pain in her eyes was still very apparent. We put our foreheads together for a brief second then my mother took my hand and led me into her bedroom to the hatch of the tunnel under a rug that lay on the floor by her bed. She opened it then came to me again. "I need you to promise me that no matter what you hear, no matter what is done to me, promise me that you won't stop. You just keep running."

"I promise," I said with a heavy heart. Just then the door thundered from fierce fists as they hollered in Italian for my mother to open the door. My mother kissed my forehead and sent me on my way. She shut the hatch and locked it. As soon as she laid the rug back down straight, I could hear them breaking down the front door.

I quickly made my way to the food and supplies. I turned to our horse. He was a beautiful Clydesdale. His dark brown cote shined even at night along with his very long pitch-black hair. He had white along his belly and at the ankles. He was calm and staring at me. I couldn't help but feel like he knew more than I did. I could hear them asking her where I was so I quickly strapped as much as I could on him while I choked down the tears and bottled up the panic that pounded loudly all over my body, inside and out. I slowly snuck the horse out of the stables and through the small corn field behind the stables. When we got out of cornfield I hopped on then said, "Run like the wind, Marco." As soon as that was said, he sprinted off.

I heard someone from the mob shouted, "There goes her demon seed now!" The others were shouting at my mother and accusing her of horrible things. Then she began to scream. I wanted to turn around; I wanted to try and do something, but I had a promise to keep and now they were chasing me.

The Underground

Marco took me deep into the forest. I could tell that he was getting tired and probably dying for food and water. I brought him to a halt when I could hear men on horses in the distance behind me. I got down and rearranged a satchel for me to carry on foot. "I have to do this on my own now. It will be easier for me to hide. You've done well. Now go… be free," I said to Marco. He nudged my cheek and I hugged him then he ran off.

I wasted no time and started running deeper into the forest. The ground was rough with broken twigs and small rocks that scratched at my bare feet, but I kept running. I ran until I could no longer breathe and my legs wobbled from weakness. Tired, hungry, and seemingly lost, I stopped to lean against a tree. My mouth was dry, my throat scratched from my fast paced hard breathing and I lost what food I had somewhere along the way but going back to search was not an option.

I could hear running water not far from the tree I was leaning on. So I slowly made my way in the direction of the sound. The sun had already begun to set, and I could just barely see where I was going. Each step I took carefully, wincing at the pain of my bleeding cut and bruised feet. My body was weak with exhaustion so I stumbled. The ground beneath me suddenly slanted downward and I tripped landing face first a foot away from the edge of a creek after rolling a couple times. I pushed myself up on my hands and knees then crawled toward it. When I got to the edge, I collapsed my body and laid flat on my belly then dipped my hands in the cool water to drink.

After sipping some water, I rolled over on my back and realized that my legs were not going to allow me to get up again nor could I contain my tears of desperation any longer. I cried curling up into a ball holding onto the emerald that mother had given me. It was the only thing I didn't drop in my frantic run. I cried so hard that after ten minutes; I felt myself trying to drift into sleep. After a minute or two of struggling with myself to stay awake, I was beginning to lose the fight. My eyes felt like heavy weights and the moonlight gliding along the creek, not even a foot away from me, I couldn't see. No matter how hard I tried, I could not get my body to respond to the commands of my mind. The muscles in my legs would only twitch and my arms really weren't much help without my legs. Dragging me just did not seem like it would do me much good in the dark blanket that covered most of the forest.

It seemed that I had lost everything. Hope, faith, my home, my mother, and I doubted that Michael was going keep his promise. For me, that meant he was dead. Also I no longer had freedom in my grasps. I had nowhere I could go without being recognized and God knows what they would do to me considering that according to most I was the devil's first-born daughter. Freedom, I know was something that all can agree with me when I say, it was what it means to be human. Your soul breathes and feeds on it. Most that are deprived of their freedom are driven to the darkest realm of the madness within them. I had no one and nothing therefore I failed to find a reason to want to live.

I felt like a prisoner to the earth that lay beneath me and I hoped, no…I prayed that a ravenous bear or hungry mother wolf searching to feed her young, would find me before the mob that I thought were still behind me did. I couldn't think of anything better than to be with my mother and Michael wherever their souls had taken them. I didn't want to eat if I could and I didn't feel like trying to reach the water again so, I laid there hoping that if a bear or a wolf didn't kill me then starvation and dehydration would. Just when a deep sleep seemed to be within reach and I finally closed my eyes…the wind picked up violently then fell silent instantly. I heard leaves crunching and twigs snapping. 'Had the mob found me or were my prayers of death about to be answered?' I asked myself.

The sound became clearer as it got closer. It wasn't an animal but something I couldn't identify. Something big and heavy. The trees moaned as it worked its way past them with a nudge. The sound of a deep breathing elephant got closer. My eyes opened wide with fear and I saw an enormous black shadow that consumed the trees as its owner moved in closer.

It stopped moving and I looked around frantically. Then something caught my eye. A pair of big blue glowing eyes. They stared for a brief second then vanished. The breathing in my chest painfully got deeper and quicker from the anxiety, though my lungs struggled I could still feel them trying. I wanted to run but my body was still refusing my request to move.

Now the sound of a man's footsteps was right by me slowly trudging down the small slope I had fallen down. I could barely see a silhouette of a man stop at my side. He knelt down and I struggled to roll over in foolish hopes that I had one last run in me

"Please don't." I was able to burst out in a choked up whisper.

Suddenly I could feel the man's soft, warm, and oddly sweet breath on my ear, "Pan, I would sooner take my own life than harm you. I made a promise that I intend to keep," he whispered then shuffled his arms under my limp body and as if I was a feather, lifted me. He held me close to his steady beating heart and said softly, "Sleep. You are safe now." Of course doubt was there, yet I was comfortable, my anxiety, my fear, and all my pain seemed to have been sucked out of me with an invisible straw. It's not like I had another option or the ability to fight and run so I had no choice but to trust him. I did just that, and prayed that I wasn't dreaming.

He seemed to be moving at the speed of light. My hair swooshed around my face and the semi-cool air curved around us. It felt like we were flying. If we had been riding a horse, this horse was very light on his hooves for there was no sound of pounding on the ground. I decided to stop analyzing everything and take his advice. I finally let myself drift off to my own sweet dreams. I couldn't stay awake any longer.

My dream ended up being not so sweet though. There was fire blazing all around me. I couldn't see anything but smoke and all I could hear was my mother screaming. Then a gust of wind swept past me thinning out small section in the wall of fire and smoke around me. I peered through it not being able to make way through and there she was, my mother. She was quiet, engulfed in flames, tied to a stake, and...dead. Her body was charred and not much was left of her clothing. Suddenly her eyes shot open, her head snapped in my direction and she whispered loudly, "It's always been him." Then I woke up in a panic.

The top half of my body shot up with my eyes ready for tears and I was near hyperventilation. I plopped my body back down to pull myself back to reality. That's when I realized that I was laying on a bed and soft thin-netted blankets were surrounding it. They were black and burgundy with fine golden stitching of Celtic designs.

I felt a draft on my shoulders and out of reaction put my hand on it to rub then, I noticed that I was wearing less than I remembered. The pain in my feet was gone and I felt clean. I ran my fingers through my hair noticing that it was soft and brushed. Covering me was a heavy blanket of pitch-black fur that came from something the size of a grizzly bear. Growing up I had heard the stories of animals the size of bears, that were said to have been seen wandering all over Europe and Italy known as yes, werewolves and demon shape shifters, but that's all they were to me, just stories. I looked down to my chest and peeked under the blanket to see that it and a deep purple silk sheet under the blanket covering me to guard from the cold leather on the other side of the fur were the only things I had on.

I glided my hand down over the blanket that covered my body and to my side feeling the soft silk like hair. I looked to the fine, soft, and thin netting that hung from oak wood bed posts and oh was the carving beautiful. There was an intricate design of detailed vines carved into the posts twisting all the way up.

From the corner of my eye as I turned my head to follow the vines admirably up the post, I felt my cheek brush up along the face of my pillow. I propped myself on my side and used my elbow for a kick stand. The pillow was unlike any that I had ever seen; then again, I didn't get out much. It was round and small. The fabric was dark blue silk tightened around what I assume was cotton and, holding it together snuggly was a fine golden stitching of a star with six points that stretched into thinner lines making six sections that were bordered by a somewhat thicker gold stitching all the way around the pillow. Imbedded in the silk were symbols that I recognized from some of my mother's lessons, I couldn't remember what they were called though.

I started to get the feeling that I wasn't alone and I was right. The air shifted and the curtains hanging in front of me lightly swayed. "It's Egyptian. They're called hieroglyphs," a man said with a light but confident tone. Startled and slightly creeped out, I jolted up pulling on the sheet and holding it to my chest in one quick movement.

My eyes were wide and fixed on the male figure that stood about three feet from the bed. I couldn't see well enough through the curtains to make out a face but he was tall, maybe six feet three inches, and his build seemed thick with muscle. Something about the voice was familiar though. "I didn't mean to startle you, but I did mean what I said before…you *are* safe now," he said.

Then it hit me. "You're the one who found me?" I confirmed, relieved but still a little on guard.

I heard him snicker as if amused "I didn't have to look. I was already there…waiting in the distance," he said in a smug tone.

I could tell that this man thought highly of himself. I had a look of confusion on my face. "You knew where I was going to be?"

"Yes," he answered.

I was still confused. "Wait, are you saying that you can see the future?" I asked in mild astonishment as I situated myself and pulled the sheet to tie it around me.

"I can see anything I want, with the exception of the past."

"Who are you?"

"Your guardian angel," he answered suddenly sitting next to me. My body gave a quick shutter as I shuffled back a few inches while gripping the sheet to make sure that it stayed on.

I wasn't gonna argue the angel factor. His face was gorgeous. His skin was lighter than mine but seemed as smooth as silk. His diamond blue eyes were intensified by his perfectly shaped eyebrows. His hair was short, choppy and black as the night sky. As a matter of fact, it looked like fine strands of a starry night were cut out of the sky for his head from the way it glistened in the candlelight. The cut was an odd style to me at that time but he made it look good. There was also a goatee to accent a mild but glorious, smile that came across his face. He was amused again which I admit slightly irritated me. "Have I not earned your trust?" His smile widened and his ego shined.

"Am I really that amusing to you?" I asked, not really needing or wanting an answer. I was trying to sound as prominent as I could in a situation like this one. Gain some kind of dignity, which I think at that moment, was not possible. He giggled under his breath then stood up and glided the curtains open. "There are some clothes here on a chair for you. They should fit. Try to get ready quickly. Somebody is waiting for you to accompany them for dinner. I will be just outside the door." He made his way to the door and opened just a notch then turned. His eyes scanned my body slowly, "My name is Keyoni. Should you need any help please let me know." His eyes locked on mine, "I would be more than happy to be of…service." I glared at him and he smiled his beautiful smile then drifted out the door.

Keyoni. I thought to myself. An unusual name but fitting. There was so much running through my mind. Thinking of him only seemed to make it worse. There were so many questions. Where am I? How long have I been here? And am I really safe? The only thing that made me comfortable was that fact that my intuition was calm. Seemingly helpless and easily cornered, I was still not afraid. I did trust Keyoni to an extent, but I reminded myself to stay cautious. After all, I was just being chased by people who wanted me dead with no mercy.

I sat there for a couple minutes looking around the room. The walls were rugged with no windows and gave me the impression that this room was carved, either deep into a cave or underground. To my surprise there across from me was a cherry wood vanity with more Celtic designs carved into it. Back then only royalty owned something like that. Only the richest of kings could afford them. Mirrors were unheard of for less advantaged people like my family in a time when poverty was at its worst. I could see the clothes draped over the arm of the chair that matched the vanity. The designs of both the chair and vanity were elegant and the wood looked smooth. I decided to get up so I would not keep Keyoni waiting too long.

I carefully scooted to the edge of the bed and let my feet dangle over a hand woven throw rug that lay by the bed. The rug was also exquisite itself. I pushed up off the bed to stand with the sheet tied tightly around me and my legs began to shake. As I tried to get one leg to take a step toward the chair my equilibrium failed me. My other leg gave out, and I began to fall expecting to feel myself hit the hard ground.

As quickly as my legs gave out…there he was. Keyoni and his breathtaking face. Holding me in mid air, only inches from the ground and I realized that I was holding onto him. My hands were tightly gripping his shirt, out of natural reaction I guess. I looked away from his astonishing eyes to investigate his shirt. The shirt was odd to me. It was dark green silk, but the style was not a style from the past or present. He sure did pull it off though. His muscles were hard, well toned…a perfect body to go with a perfect head. "It will be a shirt that most men with good money and taste will be wearing all over the world... in a few hundred years," he said.

"Oh. Okay," I said a little confused, then I looked back up at him as he swooped me up in one gliding stride and held me close.

He idled for a second meeting my stare. I thought I was going to melt in his arms ruining his silk shirt. Then he said, "It seems as though you needed my assistance after all." He smiled at me like a honry child, obviously delighted with himself. I grinned innocently hoping that he didn't notice that I was lost in his eyes.

Keyoni then gently let my legs down and stood me up with him holding on gently. I was beginning to sweat against his hot-temperatured body. He felt like he was running a fever of 104 or more. Not to mention I was a little nervous. My breathing got deeper and a little faster; I couldn't help it. His touch was that of a god offering you all the pleasure in the world making it even harder to control the urge to offer everything to him.

As I rested my left arm along his arm still wrapped around the middle back, he glided the other arm up toward my upper back with his hand landscaping like a feather. He then reached across and gently tugged at the knot I tried to keep the sheet on. I slightly pushed away to stop him while whispering, "No." This was all I had enough breath left for. He carefully tightened his grasp to keep me close with his right arm. Then with his left he slid my hair back over my shoulder on the same side. Keyoni brushed his gentle hand down the back of my shoulder then dipped his head in close to my ear breathing lightly and whispered, "Don't you trust me?" There was a pause then I nodded unable to push the word out. "Close your eyes…please." I closed my eyes trying to compose myself. Keyoni reached across me again and tugged at the knot. "One…" he began, "Two…Three." The third time was more like a yank and I felt a light brush of air all over my body.

My legs felt strong and he was no longer holding on. I opened my eyes and saw myself standing in front of the mirror and then I looked up and down at myself. Yep, this was me. I looked back at the mirror and saw a beautiful girl not evil or peasant. Long, wavy, and healthy black hair and big brown eyes that had longing full lashes to add enchantment and awe to them. My skin tone was a creamy peach tone with a soft complexion.

I was wearing a black cotton dress. Fitted to curves I didn't realize I had, but not too tightly. The straps were thin at the end and thick at the shoulder with tiny black-onyx stone pieces glittering on them. The rest of the dress beyond the straps was covered by something that I knew had to be another one of Keyoni's inventions for the far future.

Black silk ribbon was crisscrossed all the way down to my waist holding together deep-forest green colored silk with more onyx pieces all over it. It was snug yet comfortable. The bottom part of the dress hung loosely off my hips and seemed wide from the extra cotton material sewn onto it making a slanting layered look. Glittering onyx pieces lined the bottom of each layer. I lifted the bottom of the dress to look at the black knee-high, two-inch-heeled leather boots with buckles. Then, I thought to myself, 'I didn't know that boots like this existed. Women don't wear boots, do they?' While looking down, I realized what was dangling from my neck. It was the amethyst necklace that Michael gave to me. I looked up at myself in the mirror and clinched the amethyst. "It was laying next you," Keyoni said

"Thank you," I said looking back at him sentimentally in the mirror. He nodded in a gesture of welcome. I looked back down at what Keyoni called a corset and lightly brushed my hands along the tiny crystal like pieces. "It almost seems a little too extravagant," I said.

"Okay," said Keyoni, then he took a step forward and in one quick motion reached at my lower back and I heard a small snap. The corset dropped to the floor.

It turned out that part of the dress underneath the corset was a lot thinner than I wanted it to be. I gasped and quickly picked it up holding it over my breasts. I shot my head to see over my shoulder and glared at Keyoni with fury. His eyes were sinister, but his smile was proud and playful. I sighed heavily and rolled my eyes turning my head back around. "Okay okay, I will get it back on for you. I just couldn't help myself," he said smiling like an angel. I gazed at him through the mirror still a little irritated, with a stone face.

"You mean you didn't want to."

"That too." Keyoni's smile widened in satisfaction of himself and his little prank, while he finished snapping the corset on me.

"Keyoni!" A woman was standing at the door looking at him crossly. She was beautiful with soft fair skin that was lightly freckled. She had an angelic face structure with dark green eyes and a fit curvy body. Her thick, straight light brown hair hung down to the back of her knees shinning like silk. She was wearing a lavender dress with sleeves that draped just below her shoulder line and flared at the wrist, hanging about a foot down. She was also wearing a deep blue corset that had small white pearls dotted on it.

"What is taking so long? He's waiting!" she said to him sternly. She walked in my direction as she glared at Keyoni suspiciously. "Are you being good?" she asked him

"Of course. We were just about to make our way to dinner," he said smugly. She rolled her eyes and scoffed then, looked at me with a much more kind and welcoming face than she gave him.

"Hello. My name is Leeana. You can call me Lee. I see you've met my obnoxious friend," she said looking back at him with a slight glare. I giggled under my breath and if I didn't know any better, it sounded like he was growling at her. I could tell that it was the kind of low growl that doesn't come from anything human or animal. He scowled at her then snickered playfully and directed his hands toward the open door. Lee looked at me, "You look stunning. Are you ready?" she asked, I nodded unsure. I couldn't help but wonder who would be waiting for *me*?

When we walked out, the candles went out and the door shut lightly without anyone touching them. "All will be explained later," Lee said. I turned to her, "Come now. A surprise awaits you." She gently put her hand on my back and directed me forward.

We walked through a long corridor carved into the earth with a couple of steps here and there. Candle lit lanterns that hung from the walls released a sweet aroma of lavender and jasmine. Keyoni kept a steady pace ahead while Lee walked by my side. They almost seemed to be gliding. My heels made clocking sounds that echoed and the back bottom part of my dress shuffled on the dirt ground. Neither Lee nor Keyoni made a sound. It was as if they were walking on clouds. So many things that my mother had taught me real and myth were coming to life for me. Sure, I can light candles without coming near them, make water boil without fire, and stir without holding the spoon. Some of the things I had been seeing, things Keyoni did, were things I couldn't do…yet. Things that my mother said she would teach me when I was eighteen, but two days was nowhere near enough time.

I was nervous and a bit scared. I had no idea where I was or who I was going to see. I even thought that I could be in more danger than when I was lying helpless in the woods. I thought of all kinds of things like a cult and I was to become their sacrifice or a feast for blood thirsty vampires. I hoped that Lee and Keyoni were as good-natured as they seemed to be. "Don't worry so much. My brother does not give false promises," Lee said, as if she could hear my thoughts.

At the end of the corridor, I could see an archway; and as we walked through it, I suddenly felt a small tingle rush through my body as if someone had walked right through me. The strange thing was that it comforted me. I stopped and looked over my shoulder to try and see if anybody did walk through me. Nothing was there. Lee gently took my hand and guided me onward. "It's a spell for protection," she said. Her hand was hot also like she'd been boiling it in water. I landscaped the round large room. It was well lit by a large candle chandelier and had beautifully strange furniture from all around the world. There were tapestries that were rich in colors of blue, deep purple, red, gold, silver, and more. There were trinkets made of wood, stone, silver, and gold. Some were shaped like gods and goddesses and some were just random animals and symbols that only a few I could recognize. We stopped in front of two doors that had tall and wide cherry wood-framed mirrors on each side. Mirrors placed at an entrance are believed, by some, to reflect away evil, and the mirrors were also pointed in the direction of the archway.

Keyoni gracefully stepped toward the door and opened it. "Ladies first," he said smiling lightly.

I blushed looking down and then Lee said, "Beauty before age." She gestured toward the open door. I looked at the entrance unsure of what I was about to walk into. The air shifted and a couple of strands of my hair slightly danced with it then fell back down. I could feel Keyoni standing close behind me.

"We're right behind you," he whispered softly in my ear. I could hear Lee lightly slap the back of his head. His breath was like lilacs in the summer breeze. I think I stopped breathing, because I felt the need to take a deep breath before entering the next room.

The room was filled with chamber music and happy soft voices. A bright light shined through the railing and pillars on one side then flickered with the shadows on the wall of the other side. Down in front of me was a long curved stairway. I kept walking feeling the nervous tension in me crawling back up my spine. 'Just keep going. Remember, you are safe.' I kept telling myself as I watched my feet take every step closer to the last.

When I got to the bottom and planted myself at the end of the steps. I looked around at all the people. The women were all beautiful and elegantly dressed along with some of the men. Some men were a little rough, but good looking nonetheless.

Then I realized that they were all looking at me. The room fell silent and for a second, time seemed to be standing still. I quickly scanned the ballroom sized space and all the people. In the back a little to my left I could see someone moving in my direction. It was a man, tall, and buff, with jet-black hair. He stopped about fifteen feet in front of me standing still behind a few people that parted like the red sea. The man stepped a couple feet closer.

My eyes widened. I knew him. But was it him? I tilted my head a little and scanned him too. He seemed different, but just as doubt came to mind, I saw his eyes. I gasped straightening my head. Tears filled my eyes as he came closer and stopped only a foot away from me.

"Michael?" I choked out. He grinned widely

"Hi, Pan," he said calmly. I jolted toward him throwing my arm around his rock hard body. Michael curled his arms around me and kissed the top of my head. I squeezed his rock solid cold body as hard as I could manage.

"I thought you were dead." I sobbed not caring about why his skin was so pale and cold.

"I am sorry. I sent Keyoni for you because he is much stronger and faster than I am. I know you are confused, but I hope that you can find some comfort within you knowing that I am here now." I took a step back and looked at him with sorrow.

"Momma…she's…I couldn't she made me promise! I'm sorry," I said still sobbing. Michael came to me and put both hands on my face and bent forward slightly to my level.

"There was nothing that you could have done without getting yourself killed and that would have disgraced Momma. She was ready and proud to give her life for yours, as am I." Michael spoke softly then smiled. A feeling of comfort, seeming to come from his cold yet firm and rugged hands, flushed through my body. All the sorrow within me washed away. Well, at least for now.

Michael went over to Lee still standing about three steps up the staircase behind me. Michael put one foot on the first step and stretched out his arm holding out his hand for hers. Lee took his hand and glided down the steps. Then they carefully embraced each other with a small but sweet kiss. Michael looked over at Keyoni leaning against the wall to the left at the bottom of the steps. He held out his hand and smiled. Keyoni stepped toward him and shook Michael's hand, "Thank you brother. You kept your word and for that I am grateful." Michael said to him.

Keyoni gave a nod and said, "Please, don't thank me yet. When I made that promise I gave her a lifetime of servitude. As long as I live she will always be safe." Michael gave a nod back at him then came over to me.

"What promise is he talking about?" I asked Michael.

"You really need to learn how to relax. Trust me. I will explain everything later."

Later…I was getting tired of hearing that word. Michael put one arm on my back then leaned over, "They've all been waiting a lot longer than you could ever know to finally meet you. This is your home now. Get comfortable and try to be sociable." Michael took Lee's hand, "Keyoni would you mind staying with Pan and please try to make her feel comfortable if you can?" Michael asked.

Keyoni looked at Lee and grinned devilishly, "Sure, I would love to," he said then Lee glared at him as she put her arm around Michael's and slowly turned her back to him as they started to make their way toward the crowd.

"Are you sure that's a good idea?" I heard Lee asked.

"Yes. She needs that kind of attention right know. It'll be a good distraction."

"I don't trust him."

Michael smiled then said, "That's because he's unpredictable and uncontrollable so that bugs you." Lee shot her head back at Keyoni and glared intensely then turned her head back around and kept going.

Keyoni smiled in victory then stood in front of me as godly as ever. His smile turned back into a mischievous small grin as he noticed that I was, yet again, mesmerized by him and his stunning eyes. Keyoni took my hand. I felt a slight shutter ripple quickly up and down my spine and it showed. He fully smiled, "Shall we?" he asked rhetorically then walked me over to the crowd.

Everyone surrounded themselves around me and introduced themselves. One by one they came. Every race of men and women. Some dressed in styles that I had never seen in person. They all told me how excited they were to finally meet me. What did they mean by finally? I thought to myself. I assumed that Michael had been talking about me. What I didn't understand was why all the excitement? Like I said before, anyone who tried to get close to me had died except for Michael. My confusion was causing frustration to emerge and I think Keyoni noticed. I stood in the middle of a small crowed trying to stay as polite as I could be. Keyoni was standing by me and I heard him inhale slowly then beautiful slow chamber music began to weave through the ballroom as he exhaled.

Keyoni stood in front of me breaking all of my concentration. "Will you dance with me?" he asked holding out his hand. I needed to break away from the congestion so without hesitation I took his hand. He pulled me close.

"Thank you." I said. Keyoni grinned.

"This is the only time that they will be like this. Like Michael said, they have been waiting a long time," he said. Then he lightly held me close. I rested my head on his chest and exhaled slowly. I wanted to ask so many questions but dancing with him was pure bliss, and I didn't want to think of anything or anyone else at the moment. My mind was finally calm as long as I was with him.

After a couple of hours of dancing, conversation, food, and drink at the biggest table I had ever imagined could be created; Keyoni went over to Michael sitting in a chair that overlooked everyone and whispered something to him. Michael nodded and then gestured for Keyoni to come closer so he could whisper something back to him. I tried to read his lips but couldn't. Michael looked up and spotted me watching them intensely. I have to admit, I was waiting for the bad news. The point when the vale was lifted to reveal the terrifying truth. Little did I know; the truth was worse than I thought it would be. My world was about to go for a radical spin.

Michael stood and came over to me smiling contently, though shown a spark of worry. I smiled back hoping that he couldn't see the anxiety from my confusion. I needed answers and he knew it. He held out his hand and said, "Come with me. There's something I want to show you." I took his hand and looked past him up at Keyoni. He was seated and staring at me then he smiled and the volcano of my anxiety cooled.

Michael led me back the way we came telling me a story from one of his adventures. It was an amazing story. Keyoni was Michael's first stop and though it seemed to Michael that he was never going to find him after eighteen months of searching; he heard a scuffle in the distance one evening and went to see what going on when he saw Lee outnumbered and surrounded. Taken by her unforgettable beauty, he risked his life to try and save her from what turned out to be three vampires. One of them struck Michael down and bit him. Keyoni swept in and ended it. As thanks for his great risk; Lee had Michael drink some of her blood to at least kill the thirst for blood and cleanse the evil in the venom. Michael and Keyoni had been great friends since then and Lee had been his only true love. It sounded like a fairytale, almost unbelievable, but I couldn't think of a reason why he would lie like that. He never lied to me before.

The First Seven

Michael led me into a room at the other end of the long corridor. "Do you remember the stories about the dragons? The good and the bad, the vampires, shape-shifters, and werewolves?" Michael asked as he steadily walked ahead of me toward a book that, from the looks of it, had been around since time began for mankind. Its cover was made of brimstone with carefully carved symbols and a woman in the middle of it nurturing an infant in one arm and holding high a globe.

I recognized a lot of the symbols from our mother's schooling and I put two and two together. I stopped just two feet behind Michael and looked at him in awe and confusion then answered, "Yeah?" He turned to me. "The nights you came to me with your dreams and nightmares? They were more than that. They were premonitions and memories. I am sorry for making you think otherwise, but the things you were seeing were too hard for me to explain. You were so young. You would not have been able to understand. That's why I am going to tell you now. It'll be a little shocking but keep that mind Momma raised you with, an open mind."

Oh god, do I even wanna know? I thought to myself. I looked at him confused though deep inside I was more afraid than anything. But I did need to know because I wanted to understand.

"Those stories and premonitions were all real. The dreams were memories of your past lives and present. The nightmares were premonitions of the future, near and far. The stories....Momma picked certain stories to educate you."

I giggled then said, "Michael, come on be serious." His face was expressionless. "You are being serious aren't you?" I said wide-eyed with amazement.

"Come here. I want to show you something," Michael said. We walked over to a curtain that hung on his wall. Michael glided the curtain aside to reveal a dimly lit round room.

The floor was designed with pieces of tile that were put together with precision to make another six pointed star like the one on the pillow. Each point of the star had a stand at the end of the point against the wall with very large books on them and hanging above them were paintings. The first painting that caught my eyes was the one of an angel then just from first glance the rest of the paintings were obvious; a demon, a werewolf, a vampire, a dragon, and a warlock. In the middle of the star was a slightly bigger more elegant stand with a book that was much larger than the other six. The book was simple, held together with leather laced down its spine and a wooden front and back cover with a Celtic trinity knot carved into the front cover. A chandelier hung from the ceiling directly over the book in the middle, shaped like the pentagram with a candle at each point and a bigger candle in the middle. "You have become quite the collector. It is an odd collection but interesting," I said, looking around the room.

Michael said nothing then walked over to the book in the middle, put his hand on it and looked at me still standing near the doorway. "This is *The Book of Eternity*." I slowly stepped in and walked over to the right side of Michael to see the book.

"Most believe that the Bible was the first religious book to have ever been written." He continued. "Well most don't even know this book exists not even the Vatican knew about this one and the few who did, vanished centuries before the bible was even thought of. This book holds the key to all known and unknown life to have ever existed. Religion, medicine, war, majick, herbal practices, and the history of the world fill a lot of these pages. The exact date of its creation isn't clear but we do know that it is about sixty-one thousand years old. It was written by the first seven Mystics that had created and spawned true immortality. There are seven chapters of 187 pages making a total of 1,313 pages."

I realized the pattern seven books and seven chapters; I stepped over to Michael and said, "13–13?" Michael nodded, "Each one had a different view on the world and how they wanted to be a part of it. In finding immortality, the six each used it differently, but the seventh combined it all. The immortality resided in an elixir that not only gave them the ability to live forever but to live forever in whatever form they chose. The abilities were different though. They could only have thirteen at the most and taking another's soul was out of the question.

The first wished to be a warrior saint to the gods with the ability to not be seen or heard and to fly at the speed light."

"The angel," I said pointing at the painting.

"Yes. The second being born of darkness in their heart wished to become a soldier of evil also with the ability to not be seen or heard and wished to be able to possess the human mind of the wicked and the freedom to choose sides at any time, which was the demon. The vampire and the werewolf wished to be guardians to the mystic; one to guard over night and one to guard from dawn to dusk with the abilities of amazing strength, wisdom, and invincibility. The warlock chose to be the one who would keep order of the balance between our world and the supernatural world. He was also given all of the greatest wisdom of the universe. The sixth wished to be more powerful than them all. He could defeat any enemy, burn down an entire forest in seconds, shape shift, fly at warp speed, see the present and the future, and was an irresistible force to be reckoned with. They're for making it possible for him to get his way through out his entire existence. The other six books are their individual history written by them and added to by their descendants."

"If they are immortal…what happen to them?" I asked.

"The world had changed and not for the better. Over the years, more people had become uncomfortable with vampires requiring blood to live; and eventually, Christian and Catholic alike began to hunt vampires. The first vampire went to the werewolves for protection. Then after enduring so much hate which was powered by fear; the first vampire had succumbed to his dark side. He decided to start a war with mankind. Basically it would be a battle for existence.

He went to the first werewolf with his plan but the werewolf disagreed and pulled back most of his protection. Some wolves strayed and agreed with his plan. The vampire was angry by the leader's decision so a war between them broke out that had become not just their war but the world's also. It got to a point where it was no longer about them. It had quietly lasted through the years as a war between good and evil. Who would inhabit the earth? Humanity had become all too familiar with them and their weaknesses. They were tiered of the war spilling into their homes.

Naturally after a while it wasn't just the Christians and Catholics that were hunting them. The warlock, the angel, and the dragon came up with a plan to separate the worlds. With intent on veiling the supernatural realm so that it would not be seen by the human eye. They have become very skilled in staying hidden."

"What about their descendants?" I questioned.

"Too many to explain them all, but I can tell you that everyone you met down there are full-blood descendants of all but one... the dragon. He had no known descendants. But that is a story for another time. Soon a lot more will come. Human descendants who are half-bloods of combined mystic abilities," Michael answered then continued on, "the oldest and most powerful descendants each have unique abilities and some abilities that are the same for all. For most, everything will eventually fade into nothing and just die from being ignored and unused. Leaving just one ability to be had." I looked at him in question. "You ever wonder why the soul is indestructible?" he asked and I gasped putting one hand over my mouth.

"Oh my god," I whispered then slowly lowered my hands.

"None of it was ever possible though without…" Michael paused and then opened the book to the last chapter, "The seventh," he said. I stepped closer to look. My mouth dropped. On the first page of the last chapter was water-painted picture of a woman that looked exactly like me. I stared in amazement.

"She was the one born of both worlds. Not sure yet again of when, but it is safe to assume that it was no more than twenty thousand years ago," Michael began. "She was born with all the abilities that the others had and more. She is their creator. Her mother was an angel, one of the God's first angels. Her father was—"

"A demon," I interrupted wide eyed still looking at the painting and now wondering how I knew that.

"Not just a demon but the first. Their love was forbidden and their child was a threat to both the heavens and hell. The child had the best of the gods and the best of hell's evil, therefore, neither one side could soley govern her. So they were cast away to earth in human form with their immortality stripped away from the angel and demon but not the child. The child was given a gift. A gift that all beings had, but with the powers combined, hers became stronger. The gift of freewill meaning only she could decide the fate of her own soul when death came knocking. No matter what."

"Why did the gods did not strip her?" I asked Michael.

"It was against their natural laws. The child was also an innocent and their laws say that makes her untouchable.

Her parents loved her to the fullest and taught her everything they knew. They knew just about everything on both sides. One day though, she witnessed the evil that hells minions influenced in men by having to watch her parents die in a tiny yet brutal battle with two other men who were possessed and sent to kill them all while they were traveling. One of the men died in the fight after her father, in his last breath, ran a spear through him. The other came for her after finishing off her mother. She tried running but he was faster. He knocked her down and tried to have his way with her. She saw a sharp tipped stick lying next to her and shoved it through his neck. He screeched a blood gurgling scream and the demons rose out of the bodies then fled. The man choked on his own blood as he looked at her struggling to understand why he had been murdered. Then his body went limp on top of her. She shoved him off her and got up quickly then ran. When she couldn't run anymore she wandered hours with the pain of guilt and terrible loss before a woman tending to her corn, witnessed her pass out in the field. She was only twelve. The woman took her in and raised her just as well.

From the moment that man died, it damaged her innocence, which was the plan. The murder was still innocent though. She was defending herself and the gods knew what hell was trying to do, so that fine line still allowed her to be safe from the god's harsh judgment but not from evil.

Premonitions about the future of mankind's existence poured in and were getting worse. More and more horrific violence to come raced through her head. One night when she was fifteen, Lucifer came to her in her sleep with a new plan and a truce. He realized he could not control all of the evil souls that would inhabit hell over time. He warned of the battle for earth and that mankind would fall to oblivion under no one's control, unless she tipped the scale. She was the only one that could. So that night, she vowed with her soul that she would take the human existence in a different path, no matter how long it took. One way or another, even if it is only a few, humanity would be saved and start new. Not for the god's benefit but for all humankind, the good, the kind, the humble, the meek, the poor, the honest fighters, the true lovers, and the protectors of innocence. She would remind the strong willed of true love and hope. She promised to strengthen mankind in their fight for salvation. Her story had been told before, but the truth of it had long been forgotten. It has been twisted and added too. She is now known as the Antichrist and most think she…is a he."

"Wha…hold on…just stop there for a minute. Why does Lucifer care about what happens to us?" I asked, completely lost on that one.

"Unlike us, he had to do what he is told and his job is to keep the evil dead. He had a hard enough time controlling what he's got. Do you think he wants to run a world overflowing with them? If all of humanity falls and evil triumphs; the gods will force him to take control over the slop. Besides he's not totally heartless." Michael answered.

"Oh. Makes sense. Continue," I said giving a nod then Michael went on.

"It would take ten years for the plan to come into full effect. On the night of her twenty-fifth birthday, Lucifer came to her again with a way to do it as many times as she wanted to, with help in her absence also. He told her that the six people who were constant in her life; he drew them to her because they could help. She gathered the six people: a lover, fighter, friend, wise man, brother by bond, and a sister by bond. They all hesitantly agreed because the bad side to Lucifer's plan was the elixir that would give them their immortality and power; it had to be made from her blood…all of it. She was more than willing to sacrifice this and chose reincarnation. She comes back whenever the world is in most peril and/or inches too close to total destruction. Like now, the Dark Age."

Michael looked at me as if hinting something and it hit me. "No. Michael Porchillo, what kind of joke are you playing at?" I grinned but saw in his eyes that he was as serious as death. His silence was uncomforting. "No! There is no way! That's not me! I don't have any special powers. Just the stuff that Momma taught me. I…I'm just me! Just existing like everyone else." My mind began to spin and my heart was racing. Every ounce of my blood tingled. I just couldn't believe it. I paced back and forth breathing heavily.

"Pan," Michael began as he stood in front of me and put both hands on my shoulders to bring me to a halt, "Look at me. Momma was not teaching you those things. You already knew them. Momma was teaching you how to control the power within you. Our stepfather was a demon possessed human. I put belladonna in his drink like Momma instructed. The others that died were just more clever deceptions in the form of friendship and kindness. Evil wants you and if they get you…the gods will no longer be in control and the earth will burn along with all living beings. You would be their greatest weapon. Momma and I could not let it happen. So I did what I was born to do…protect you," Michael said.

I looked at him in shock. "You killed them! And worse, you let everyone believe it was me! That I was cursed! How do you know what they were?" I stepped back away from Michael and glared at him as

I crossed my arms waiting for an answer. "They killed Momma and would have killed me!" I shouted.

Michael's eyes teared up. Michael stepped forward with a jolt trying to hold back his own pain, "What was I suppose to do! Confess? Do you realize what would've been done to me! To all of us! Would you wish that on us? Pan, please try to understand. Those things were gonna kill you! They found a way to get a hold on your soul when you die. We just haven't figured how yet," Michael pleaded.

"What do you mean, we? And why would Momma love someone like that?" I asked still holding my glare at him while trying to control the panicked confusion inside me that was tearing up my heart.

"Because she didn't know what he was until months later! Deception is what they do best and he seemed as he was…to good to be true. The first mystic, the angel, came to her in her dreams when she was seven-months pregnant and revealed everything to her. Momma didn't want to believe it either, but then she found his book. A book of the purist form of evil black majick, and it made sense why a young handsome man like him would take a single pregnant pagan as his wife after only a month of knowing her, with it being frowned upon so much. Momma knew what she had to do. Her body is gone but she had been here the whole time! Pan…" Michael stepped close and I stepped back.

"No, Michael! That is not me! I cannot do any of those things!" I said in a raised and frustrated tone. I stepped back slowly then turned and walked out swiftly.

The confusion clouded my mind, the tears blurred my vision, and the painful panic made me hot. I started to run. If I am that than why didn't I know that? What if it was all just a dream that Momma had? Did those people die for nothing? Oh I had so many more questions on my mind but I couldn't gather my thoughts enough to talk anymore. This stuff doesn't happen. They are just stories, fairytales and everyone has lost their minds. Then why do I have this unnerving feeling that it is all true. I thought I made my way fast pace through a corridor.

I suddenly realized that I was lost…again. I couldn't remember were my room was nor was I sure if I wanted to stay. Just then I lost my footing and tripped over myself. Like I said, heels were a bad idea.

As I landed I hit my head on a rock sticking out of the wall knocking myself unconscious.

I slipped into my own realm of thoughts and dreams; everything within me that I could claim came before me. Any memory of everything I have ever done were mixing with others that I didn't recognize. I also got more than I bargained for. Memories of another childhood, but they weren't all mine. Some of these memories belonged to another. Unclear visions of battles were coming through. I was fighting, I think but I know I killed. It was all coming together. Maybe I am her…she is me. Could I really be of both worlds? Where else would these memories be coming from?

When I started to come to; I heard Keyoni's unquestionably mesmerizing voice. He had a deep yet soft voice with an Icelandic accent "You know…I'm beginning to think that you shouldn't be left alone. As clumsy as you are I'm afraid you might accidentally kill yourself," he said in a sarcastic tone. I slightly opened one eye and glared. Keyoni sat by my side and smiled. I opened both eyes rolling on my side so I could look away while I tried not to smile. Keyoni then put his hot hand on my head and caressed my hair. The heat from his hand warmed my body. I rolled back over to look at him and then he leaned his upper body on mine suddenly holding me. As quickly as he moved it surprised me, but I got over it quickly staring into his eyes.

I wanted him to kiss me and touch every inch of my quivering body. He closed in and then whispered in my ear, "You know you're never gonna get anywhere if you keep letting your fear chase you around in circles," he said. Then he slightly lifted his body to look into my eyes. I carefully pulled myself together and opened my eyes. Keyoni grinned seductively.

"Are you okay?" he asked as he sat back up by my side.

"Yeah, I'm just worried. I don't know what to do. I felt much safer in my head just being me. Now you all want me to open a door that will change everything." I stretched my arms a little above my head then sat up slightly leaned back holding myself up with my arms. My sheet slid down and I noticed that the corset was off. Next thing I knew, Keyoni was behind me snapping on the corset going up my back slowly. He pulled my hair over my right shoulder brushing his fingers along the back of my neck then he tightened the corset just enough for the last couple snaps and said so soft in my left ear with his sweet intoxicating breath, "Is that too tight?" I slowly shook my head no. For a second I think I stopped breathing again.

Boom, boom, boom! I jumped and Keyoni was gone. I got up quickly and went for the door. "Keyoni! If you…" Lee began then I opened it.

"Oh. Hi, hun," Lee said letting herself in. "He was here wasn't he?" she asked overlooking my room.

"Uh…"

"I can smell him," she said looking over at the bed. Lee turned to me then smiled. I noticed she was holding a package wrapped in hemp cloth. "I had these made especially for you," Lee said handing me the package. I walked over to the bed, laid the package down and began to unwrap it. "They're not what you're used to, but they're comfortable. You don't have to wear it all the time. Now if you wouldn't mind, I would love to see if it fits right," she continued as I held up another corset. It was made of hemp and leather died black with a leather string crisscrossed down the front. What baffled me were the leather pants. Why did she want me to put on men's pants? At least I thought they were men's pants. Although they did seem quite small and oddly shaped, "I will let you be and come back soon to check on you," Lee said smiling bright then she gracefully stepped out the door letting it close just as graceful behind her.

As soon as the door latched, I turned to the clothes and jumped gasping. Keyoni was standing right in front of me. He smiled devilishly. "I'm sorry," he said.

I rolled my eyes. "No you're not." I wanted to give it more attitude and just step past him but I couldn't. His unbelievable eyes had my feet glued to the floor. He smiled playfully as he gently wrapped his arms around me then leaned in. His soft lips touched mine gently but not all the way. They lightly grazed along mine and were amazing. They felt like I was being teased with rose petals. I could feel a powerful energy flooding through my veins, and I'm pretty sure that my bottom lip quivered a little. Butterflies pulsated in my stomach. My heart felt like it was shuttering when he caressed my hair and pressed his body against mine. His firm right hand rested on my lower back and gripped some of my long hair while the other hand gently slithered up my back. I curled my arms around his neck and could feel him overflowing my mind. I thought I was going to explode with lust. His body temperature boiled within me as I yearned for him to press his lips on mine. He lowered the hand that was holding my hair then loosened the corset and just as I thought we were finally to seal a kiss, he quickly disappeared taking my dress with him.

I spun around my eyes wide with confusion. I was dressed in the clothes Lee had given me. There was a gentle knock on the door. "Are you dressed?" Lee asked.

I rolled my eyes in thought of Keyoni's mischievous sense. "Uuuhhh. Yes. Yes I'm dressed." Lee slowly nudged the door open and popped her head in then a smile lit across her face.

She gave the door a shove, and it slowly swung open the rest of the way as she pranced in far more gracefully than I could ever be. "Oh it looks perfect on you. How does it feel?" Lee asked thrilled with herself.

"It feels like it fits," I said. Lee pursed her lips together.

"It's still stiff isn't it?" she asked.

I nodded and said, "A little."

"Ooooo…I told him to take care of that! It's hard to focus in the heat of battle when you're uncomfortable. Oh well, it will loosen up," Lee said in a frustrated tone.

I looked at her unbelievably confused. "Battle?" It hit me that Lee most likely didn't know that I ran out on Michael before he could tell me anymore.

"Oh. You took off before he got to that part didn't you?"

Lee took my hand and sat me down with her on the edge of my bed. "I'm gonna make this short and to the point. Nobody wishes for this kind of stuff. But unfortunately, we are only given three choices: good, evil, or nothing at all. It is all true and you are that powerful. The only thing left for you to do is decide on how you're going to use it. Will you help destroy what good in hope, love, and faith there is left, will you do nothing at all and just lay with the rest to die, or will you stand and fight?" Lee looked at me not expecting an answer.

My eyes began to water as I tried to fight back my tears, then she kissed my forehead gently with her feather soft plush lips and added,

"When you make your decision just open the door and someone will take you to Michael." Lee elegantly glided out with the door slowly closing behind her.

I knew what she was trying to do, and it was working. The way Momma raised me I couldn't hurt anyone that didn't deserved it. I couldn't just sit back letting Michael and the others die because I let fear get the best of me. I felt like I was going to explode. I hated having to make this decision, but I knew it was what I had to do.

I threw myself back on my bed, and my necklace jingled. I looked at it then picked up the crystal and examined it remembering that night in the clearing. I realized that my decision was simple. Even though I had not seen much of the world worth fighting for...the one thing I had was the true love of a family and strong feelings for a beautiful man I barely knew. Love was worth fighting for and I could not disgrace my mother in all the sacrifice she made out of her love for me.

"Life isn't about getting what you want when you want it. It's about working for what you want, earning what you deserve, and fighting for what you love," Keyoni said. I sat up quickly a little less startled than usual. I was kind of getting used to him popping in and out. I sat up half way leaning back on my elbows. "My mom used to say that." Keyoni half smiled then sat next to me at the edge and I sat up the rest of the way.

"Any good true natural and supernatural practitioner knows this saying. It's pretty old," he said. "I'm just afraid of letting everyone down. It's a lot of pressure." I looked down at my boots trying to pretend that I was studying them in hopes that Keyoni wouldn't notice the fearful tears beginning to form in my eyes.

"You can't fail at something your good at. Then you wouldn't be good at it. Why do you think we're going to train you? You didn't really think that we were just gonna throw you in it and wish you the best of luck?" he said. I smiled in realizing he was right; if I knew what I was doing, I would probably feel a lot better. That is, if I am what they say.

I looked up to his face and dazed into his tantalizing eyes then said. "Well, why are you still sitting there? I got some training to do," I said grinning playfully.

Keyoni smiled then stood and held out his hand gesturing to help me up. I placed my hand in his and he slowly pulled me close with his other hand gliding to my lower back along the waistline. I suddenly felt hypnotized and began to feel hot again. He slowly bent his head downward and I instantly turned my head to the side slowly stretching out my neck to be revealed. I don't think I could handle more teasing. He breathed lightly on my neck then quickly let go and was at the door holding it open. I stumbled a little trying to gather myself. I put my hand on my forehead to see if I was still blazing hot then shot a glare at him. Keyoni smiled mischievously. "Ladies first, love," he said standing outside of the door holding out his hand. I huffed once then rolled my eyes knowing that it would be impossible to stay mad at him much longer than five minutes.

In a smaller room with a plain wooden table that could seat no more than four, Keyoni and Lee sat me down and began to explain the training process. "This is not going to be the kind of training you could ever imagine," Lee began. "You will have new memories, new understanding of the things you have learned, and more knowledge than anyone else alive. Including combat and war strategy," she said with a wink.

Keyoni leaned forward on the table and quickly scaled my body with his eyes. We both glared at him and he leaned back in his chair. "You'll be healthier than you've ever been, too." Keyoni began to add on, "Your body will change and it's gonna hurt, but the pain is very temporary and very worth it. You'll look and feel better. You'll be more energetic and uhhh..." Keyoni paused then, noticeably not caring if anyone saw, slowly landscaped my body with his eyes again and grinned widely, "more flexible," he finished looking deep into my eyes with his devilish grin.

"Keyoni!" Lee shouted, as she stood up quickly causing the chair to scoot back about a foot. Keyoni slightly shuttered then shot a mean glare at her. I was more startled than he was. I looked up at her too. Lee came over to me and took my hand, "Come on. Michael would like to get started if you don't mind," Lee said not letting go so I figured she really wasn't asking.

Lee led me to another room with Keyoni close behind. This room was seemingly closer to the surface since moonlight was making its way through little holes in the ceiling. Michael sat on the floor next to a circle made of large, clear quartz crystals, tiger's eye and black onyx stones. In the middle of the circle was a giant pentagram lined out with pure salt. At the end of each tip on the star was something each representing the five main elements; Sage was for protection and to represent earth, a large clam shell with water in it to represent, well of course, water. A purple candle for psychic enhancement and to represent fire, a stone carved in the hieroglyphic symbol meaning air or wind, and a small brass and gold bowl to represent metal. There were candles all over the room outside of the circle.

Michael was lighting the last candle then finishing his incantation for cleansing and blessing the circle, he stood up. "This is kind of a small room for training isn't it?" I asked Michael. Keyoni chuckled a little then cleared his throat.

He then passed by me in the direction of an altar and Michael snickered. "This is a different kind of training. So…am I forgiven?" Michael asked as a grin unfolded. I smiled and nodded. "You left before I could finish so I will continue. Before the seventh died she and the other six developed this." Michael held a tiny vile in his palm with tiny medal cut and welded to the bottom. And its tiny knob of a lid was medal carefully holding a small emerald the shape of a teardrop. The liquid in side was radiating a deep red color.

"This is the elixir that you will need to bring it all back to you. Everything you knew you had and everything you never imagined you would have. You and the other six mystics created this because the human mind has never held the capacity to be able to handle memories of more than one life at a time. So we are born with no possible recollection of any of our past lives. Of course there are some exceptions. The one that Momma sent me after is still lost. It was made as sort of a failsafe. Just in case all else is lost. The world will need miracles, even small ones. That elixir will give you the most powerful indestructible immortality ever with and extra gifts that only you could ever have. If you feel you're done you may choose to end your immortality or a successor to give it to if any ever deem worthy of it whenever you see fit."

I stared at the bottle mesmerized and scared. What if my mind didn't have the capacity they thought it did? I slowly reached for it and put it in the palm of my other hand. I continued to stare.

Keyoni stood very close behind me, "This is where you come in. This is where you will decide who you are, and who you want to be," Keyoni spoke calm and seductively.

"That's cheating. She needs to make this decision on her own, without any influences," Lee said then clinched her teeth together and again I could've sworn that I heard growling.

Keyoni shot a glare over at her, "She is perfectly capable of making her own decisions either way," he said in a growling tone. I could feel the tension and the room seemed to get hotter instantaneously.

"Okay. I'm ready," I said. The tension broke and the room got cool again. All eyes were on me. I looked at Michael and a big smile had stretched across his face paved with pride and relief.

"I don't want to leave you alone with him, but Keyoni is the only one who can do the ceremony. So," Lee said then shot a glare at him, "You better be good."

Lee opened the door. Michael came closer to me. "This won't be easy but know that you're in good hands," he said. I nodded then he kissed my forehead and walked over to Lee. She reached out her hand and he took it softly as they walked out with the door closing behind them.

I turned to Keyoni and was immediately taken by his eyes. He stood on the other side of the pentagram and stretch out his hand. I couldn't say no so I put my hand in his. "Now step lightly into the middle with two steps," he said guiding me as I did what he asked. Keyoni stepped in now facing me. I gave up on self-control and bluntly star gazed into his eyes. He smiled. *Oh please be still my heart.* I thought to myself. Keyoni took one step pulling me closer with one step also. I gulped my heart back down to my chest.

"Now close your eyes," he said caressing my face lightly with two fingers. I slowly closed my eyes. Keyoni then elegantly spun me around and wrapped his arms around my waist gently pressing his body against mine, still standing in the same spot. "I know that your mother schooled you well in meditation. I want you to completely black out your mind. In doing so, drink the elixir then open your mind more than you ever have before and I'll be here, holding on," Keyoni said gently tightening his arms. "No fear," he whispered close to my ear. Being against his body was like sitting next to a bonfire but felt good

I cleared every last thing that could have ever been there. All memories of the past and present. All fantasies and feelings, everything was gone, so I lifted the vile to my lips slowly then tipped it like a shot. I cupped the empty vile in my hand then descended into the open. It all started coming back to me like I ran into a brick wall at high speed. Millions of memories from a few lifetimes. I also gained skilled knowledge and memories of great battles, wars, and one-on-one combat. The new knowledge even included ancient and unknown origins of fighting styles. Just as soon as the knowledge exploded my mind, pain that I have never known and wouldn't wish on another soul came. I understood why Keyoni was holing on. I gripped his arms half curling forward then shot back slamming into his body and I let out an ear-piercing cry.

I was going through it all not just physical but mental and spiritual pain as well. I screamed and cried begging for a release. Tears were flowing like Niagara Falls. Every muscle in my body hardened like a rock and it seemed as if my flesh was being torn in more places than I can count on all fingers, both thumbs, pinkies, and toes. I could no longer stand. Keyoni's hold tightened as he laid us both down to the ground while I squirmed. There were memories of true horror, rape, torture, wounds from swords, arrows, bites, broken bones, and ripped tendons. Then there were some that seemed more like telepathic sent memories, not my own. I strained my body crying uncontrollably while I kept a very tight grip on his arms tearing holes in his sleeves and scratching at his flesh until I calmed. He didn't flinch once, not even a little.

The pain started to fade and became nothing more than just memories then came the good. But one particularly gave me the final piece to the puzzle of my desires for Keyoni. The dragon, the protector—he became more than that to her, no…to me, and I was back in his arms. I have to admit that by realizing this I became a little upset. He couldn't tell me that before. That would've been easier to handle than anything else. The temptation and games were not necessary.

Though I had new knowledge and memories the rest of me still remained the same. According to my memories of both realms, Keyoni had been following my soul since it began its journey. The other side of me was devotedly in love with him and knew him inside and out. This side of me that lived this life hesitated from fear that made me totally unsure.

My breathing slowed and I could feel myself coming back. Keyoni was still holding on loosening his grip. His body felt like it had been dipped in lava and his deep heavy breathing began to contain itself. I opened my eyes then scooted onto my back still keeping myself close to him and Keyoni perched himself up on his side then caressed my face looking intensely into my eyes. His face was sweaty and his watery eyes were sorrow-filled with slight relief beginning to form. It hit me that he couldn't handle seeing me go through it. He could see every image, feel every emotion, and hear the explosion in my mind.

I ran my hand along his left arm remembering his ability to heal instantaneously. Not a scratch. I looked back into his eyes feeling myself set adrift in them. Suddenly my mind went blank and self-control was gone. I pulled him in and latched my lips onto his with my hand on the back of his neck. I pushed my body against his, and he embraced me sending a tingling ripple of heat throughout my body. His hand caressed my hair with his thumb skimming my cheek bone. He then pulled me up straddling me on his lap. His arms then tightened and mine coiled around him. I realized though, as his hand tantricly grazed its way down more and more, that one thing I still had no matter what was my virginity and believe it or not I was proud of it at the time. I instantly grabbed his wrist bringing it to a halt. I gathered myself and quickly peeled my glued lips off of his.

Keyoni looked at me innocently still embracing my hold. Which made it even harder, but I was not going to make this easy for him, I couldn't. A look came to his face as if he had figured it out, then he smiled stealing the air from my lungs and I knew that he knew what I was doing. A streak of amusement swept across his face and I slid off of his lap sitting on my knees as he got up then held out his hand to help me on my feet. Just as I stood, my senses turned my attention toward the door. Before she knocked I knew who it was. "Come in,"

I said in a slightly raised but calm tone. Lee carefully open the door then popped in. Her heavenly bright smile lit the room and in three gliding strides she threw her arms around me. I remembered she was the greatest friend I ever had. She is also known as the first of the six, the angel. I was compelled to hug her back tightly. I was just as excited as she was if not more. This was my first and only true friend. I no longer felt alone.

We released our hold and looked at each other then she creased her eyebrows at the distant look on my face. Sure I was excited, but there were still so many unanswered questions in my new frame of mind. All the things that resided in me were so new yet old and hard to believe that they belonged to me. Though I had gained an amazing amount of knowledge, there were quite a bit that I did not understand or came a little fuzzy to me. The first question I needed answered was about Michael. How did he fit into this? He was not in a single memory of the past except for that of my present life. I now knew the eight years he was gone was more detailed than I imagined. It took a lot to be trusted amongst the best in this kind of underground.

Lee smiled lightly, "Come with me," she said. Lee looked at Keyoni mischievously and grinned, "We'll get you away from the temptation, and I will tell you all about your brother." Keyoni rolled his eyes and gracefully made his way out the door. Lee was taking me to a place that seemed one-hundred-miles away but was only ten. I was surprised by the fact that I was not tired and out of breath from our long walk. On the way, we reminisced about the past. The battles we had won and lost. Days of peace along side with Keyoni.

"So," I began, "why hold the grudge against him?"

"Yeah you weren't aware of that one, were you?" Lee asked rhetorically then continued, "The only thing that nobody ever figured out was what would happen if you lost the one thing that gave you enough innocence left for the gods to not interfere with your fate."

I looked at her confused but also suspecting I knew what she meant, so I had to ask anyways. "What's that?"

"Your virginity. Well, the human part of it anyways," Lee answered without hesitation. It was exactly what I thought. I guess that would be why I hold my virginity so close to me.

"Keyoni's way of giving the kind of love that he has for you is physical. To him true love is mental and spiritual. The body is a magnificent conductor for combining both when you have the gift that he has for pure seduction and ecstasy. The strength in his ability to do that puts a vampire to shame," Lee said then we came to a stop. She stretched out her right hand and without saying a word a boulder for us to sit on rose up from the ground. We sat and feasted on some French bread, raspberries, and milk that she brought in a large, hemp-made satchel with an ivy leaf dyed in dark green designed on it. Holding together the button loop to keep it closed was a silver-star pendant. We chatted some more about nothing particular then when we finished our snack we thanked the gods and Lee pulled out a sage smudge stick with a clear quartz crystal that we carried for protection and awareness. I carried the sage lit in my right hand and Lee carried the crystal in her left hand and we walked on.

We arrived at our destination and Lee held up the medium-sized candle lantern we had. She handed me the crystal and I tossed what was left of the fifth sage stick that we burned. Lee climbed up a small ladder then held up the lantern to shed light on a locked hatch. She unlocked it and shoved it open. Lee handed the lantern back to me and climbed through. I shined the light so she could see where she was going then climbed up after her. When I reached the top Lee took the lantern and helped me up the rest of the way. She held the lantern above her head and I suddenly realized where we were.

It was the house that our mother lived in when Michael was a toddler and our real father was still with them. I recognized it by the fireplace that Momma had described. It was truly one of a kind just like she said. Father hand-carved four cherubs into the top of the stone fireplace and curving their way down each side he had carved roses… Momma's favorite…with amazing detail. I spaced off in amazement. Lee had found another lantern with an old dusty used candle in it. She blew the dust away and brushed of the cobwebs then lit the lantern and handed me the other one along with the satchel. I held the lantern up for good view. I could picture the life that was here and feel the warmth of the love. I began to imagine images of Momma young and happy cooking dinner while our father held Michael in his lap at the table and told him stories. The fireplace roaring with a healthy fire. I looked around at the dark house and began to feel slightly depressed.

This house was once a sanctuary of life, family, and love. My mother used use to smile regularly and everyone was safe but now… now the house is consumed with darkness and the only thing occupying it is dust, spiders and maybe a few rats or field mice. The table was rotting and there was only one chair left leaving the feeling of loneliness to mind. The broken windows added perfectly to the door that stayed on by one hinge reminding me even more of how beautiful life had all but abandoned this place. Lee put her hand on my shoulder. I snapped my head back at her in surprise. I had almost forgotten she was there. "You okay?" she asked I smiled lightly and swallowed my heavy heart.

"Yeah, I was just, looking around," I answered.

Lee walked on to the back of the house as I stopped to look up at the archway dividing the living room from the rest of the house. In the middle of it was a dusty round stained glass window. I grabbed the nearby wooden chair and stepped up on it. I reached in the satchel and found cloth to wipe the dust off the glass. I held up the lantern and realized immediately that it was the same trinity knot that was on the cover of the book. The trinity knot was green with different shades of blue surrounding it.

"Pan!" Lee called from a room in the back. I made my way in that direction and I knew exactly where she was. I could feel her energy. I could smell her aura but how? I came into the room where she was with a slightly confused look on my face. "Is something wrong?" Lee asked.

"I could feel you, almost smell you thirty feet away in another room, and it seems that no part of me knew I could do that." I said.

Lee creased her eyebrows inward in confusion then back up as if a light turned on in her head. "New powers are developing. We have to get you to Keyoni. This is unusual. Your powers have never changed before. Of course you gain more knowledge through so much time but never new powers, and he is the only one that could help figure this one out. I can't get to your inner self like that," Lee said. I noticed that a large wooden bed frame had been moved across the room and then I looked back over to Lee. She knelt on both knees and quickly rolled up a very large canvas lying where the bed was.

"What's that?"

"We'll talk about that later. Come on," Lee said and we swiftly made our way back.

A New World

Lee didn't say much and all I could do was run a billion things in my head. What does this mean? Why the urgency and why can't I remember where this came from? Everything else is so vivid and easy to identify.

"Take my hand and hold on," Lee said and as soon as I did so, it felt as if I was a stone in a slingshot that had just been viciously swung around with the speed of light then released. I pulled myself together and I saw that we were back…I think. The room was different but underground. "I know traveling like that can be kind of nauseating. You feel okay?" Lee asked. I looked at her and nodded with a half smile. Keyoni swept in and the door shut softly behind him. "Keyoni and I can telepathically communicate so I told him we were coming and why,"

I looked over to Keyoni, "So then this is your room I take it?" Keyoni nodded. It was beautifully elegant in a dark way.

"There is only one other kind in existence that has had the ability to sniff out another beings aura," Keyoni said.

"That's what worries me the most. Not to mention she has no idea how or where she got it," Lee said. I began to get worried too.

"Well, what being is it?" I asked with a concerned tone.

Keyoni looked at with hesitation then said, "A Vampire."

"Please tell me that this is some kind of sick joke." I blurted out in disbelief. Keyoni put both hands on my face drawing my eyes to his.

"Can you remember anything at all?" he asked

I just shook my head, "Believe me I tried."

Keyoni then closed his eyes and I could feel him inside my head. I closed my eyes then exhaled slowly. Keyoni dropped his hands and we both opened our eyes at the same time. He jolted his head in Lee's direction.

"Something from her memories in one of her past lives has been hazed. It was a vampire for sure. I have to take her to him, but we must leave right now," he said.

Lee nodded quickly, "Go. I'll talk to Michael." Keyoni swept me up in his arms and took off before I could ask him for details. I swear if he went any faster we would've jumped back in time to the ice ages.

The fresh and cool night air felt so good being against his body, brushing and curling around me. After a few minutes though, I began to feel nauseous and I think he knew it too. He came to a stop near a well and sat me at the base against it. I looked up at him and wanted to ask him a few questions but I didn't want to throw up on him. "Just sit here and breathe very slowly. I'm gonna get you some water," he said I nodded and didn't drop my stare for the stars caught my eye. They were so beautiful. I never knew that I would ever be this happy to see the stars in all of their blazing glory.

A shooting star blazed across the sky then disappeared as soon as it came and it made think of Keyoni's speed. I knew from memory what he looked like in his dragon form, but just the memory wasn't good enough. I wanted to experience it again then Keyoni knelt in front of me and handed me some water. I took a small drink looking at him in question. "What?" he asked.

"You can change whenever you want, right?"

Keyoni creased one eyebrow and lifted the other in wonder of where I was going with this then said, "Yeah." "Will you show me?" I asked. Keyoni smiled as if he understood with no question in his mind. He stepped back about five feet and took off like a bullet going straight up into the sky out of sight. I slowly stood up taking a couple of steps forward. The wind gust from the force of his take off whipped my hair around my face but I kept my eyes on the night sky.

The wind became more of a steady gusting whirl and the sky seemed too had been partially blacked out. I realized that he was landing. I stepped back sitting myself on the edge of the well and like the thunder of a big earthquake he shook the ground. He was on all four legs and lifted his bowed head the size of a small house to look at me. His eyes began to glow a bright lime green and were gentle looking. His black scales glistened all over with an iridescent glow of deep purple and green that even showed on his prominent horns and talons.

I slowly slipped off the well and he lowered his head down to my level. I stepped forward cautiously reaching toward him. I ran my hand on the top of his nose, in between his eyes, then down the back of his head and it seemed as if he purred. He huffed out a puff of smoke and I stood back. Keyoni then stood on his hind legs like a man with muscle bound abs and a proud chest. He fully spread his wings. His wings alone were 150 feet long, possibly more to carry his massive body. He tilted his head back and opened his mouth. Bright blue flames shot toward the heavens for only a second or two. Keyoni then bent back down to my level and held out his hand. The talons made me hesitate but I knew I was safe. I put my hand in his, which seemed like a pebble in comparison. Keyoni poked out one talon and ran the tip of it through my hair.

Suddenly his voice was in my head. "Can you hear me again?" he asked.

"Clear as fresh spring water."

"I'm going to need you to let me carry you. Please climb into the palm of my hand and hold on. The take off can be literally breathtaking. I tightly hugged his talon and buried my head in my forearm. "I have to fly you the rest of the way and I'm not sure where my clothes went," he said in my mind. I giggled and then felt a quick yet powerful gust of wind rush all over me then the air was suddenly subtle and I peeked up a little to see. I then lifted my head for better view and out of pure astonishment.

All I could think was there's no way that the take off is any more breathtaking than this. The view was unbelievably beautiful like a dream of all the most amazing things the stars could show you at once. The moon was their mother guiding them along their dancing path so full of light and life. Another reason for the right kind of inspiration… the kind I needed.

My eyes got harder to keep open but I tried. I didn't want to miss anything. I lost the battle though. My dreams had already begun to set in.

It was horribly confusing. It was as if I was inside another woman's head while giving birth in the middle of chaos with little to no time for getting away to safety. The building or house I was in was way different than any house or building around my time and the people around me were all unfamiliar to me except for one. He was just a shadowy figure but I had the feeling that I knew him. The question is how. I could not put a face or name to him yet the women seemed to feel deep love for him.

Then a flash to Keyoni holding a huge axe and swinging it at the head of a vampire. War was all around and death was having a hay day. Keyoni looked different though. He had short black hair, a goatee, and the same eye color. But his eyes were hardened and more intense. His jaw line was more distinguished and his skin tone was about the same. He was the same height with the same godly build and just as much muscle. His nose was the same but his lips were fuller and the rest of his body was covered in black ink designs, words, and pictures. The clothing really threw me off I couldn't even describe it. Even though he didn't quite look the same in my dream I knew it was him. Those eyes are unmistakable. My dream started to become more and more vivid. Pain shot through my body. Sweating and shaking followed.

I went back to the other women's mind and felt was she was feeling. I thought I was dying. In the dream I screamed and cried while squeezing the shadow figure's hands with every last ounce of my strength. She pushed and pushed but the final push sent her into a rage then we both screamed like I know I never have before. Then in the distance I could hear Keyoni's precious voice pulling me back.

My eyes shot open and I realized we had come to a stop. Keyoni had a tight hold on me his eyes wide with concern. "What happen?" he asked in a low toned voice as I wrapped my arms around his rock hard body and rested my head on his shoulder. I took a deep breath closing my eyes then exhaled slowly.

"I had a premonition…I think. I was in another women's head while she was giving birth in a time that I don't remember. I could feel her pain and it hurt worse than anything. I'm really hoping that it was just a dream." I told him then lifted my head and I pulled myself back a little to look at him.

"So you do know," Keyoni said. I looked at him suspiciously confused. "They aren't dreams one is a memory and the other is a premonition. Usually when they reoccur like that it means—"

"I know what it means and it scares me more than anything! Who is she?" I interrupted with slight panic and frustration scratching at my throat.

I lie on my back and put one arm over my eyes. Keyoni grinned, "That I do not know but it will all come back to you soon," he said with a calming tone.

It came to my attention that I was laying on a couch-like thing with one arm. I sat up and looked at it running my hand along the soft fabric with beautiful swirls that danced all over the white fabric. "These things aren't supposed to come into circulation for a long time." Keyoni smiled at my attempt to change the subject and went with it. "We aren't the only ones that can see…and invent the future." Keyoni stood and walked over to the end of the couch then grabbed a shirt to put on his devilishly delicious muscle bound body.

I was almost lost in my stare at him then came back to reality. "Where are we?"

"His name is Rahmeeku," Keyoni answered holding out one hand to help me up.

Memories flashed through my mind triggered by the name. "The warlock," I said.

The warlock was an African healer and very powerful shaman. He became a dear friend before he became a warlock. I came to him suffering from dehydration and hunger. I had been searching for days to find medicine for a sick child of a friend. He admired my strength and my will to save the life of another then offered me food and water. We visited for a little bit then he sent me on my way with a blessing and the medicine I needed. I was happy but nervous to see him at the same time. I was still struggling with this new reality.

"This life has done you better than the last. You have your mother's beauty and your fathers striking aura."

I heard a soft masculine voice say from behind me. I stood up slowly and saw Rahmeeku standing at the doorway. He was wearing a long, white silk robe with gold and silver stitching that out lined the robe and white silk pants. He had no shirt on and though his body shown to be that of a sixty-year-old man; he looked good for his actual age. He still had a soft-toned muscle structure and walked with a steady sense of pride. His chest was covered with African tribal bead necklaces. Egyptian gold symbols along with Celtic designs also hung from his neck and of course he was still barefoot. It made him feel grounded to the earth's energy. Then a memory struck me, "You knew my parents?"

Rahmeeku smiled kindly then said, "How do you think your father learned true shamanism? He was abandoned after his father died, and I took him in. I raised him with the heart of a warrior, an intelligent mind, and the soul of a good man. Then I sent him in your mother's direction. After all it's my job to make sure that things are the way they're suppose to be." I smiled knowing what he meant. We walked toward each other and stopped with only a foot of space between us. He took both my hands and then kissed my forehead. "I understand that you have been through a lot?" he asked. I nodded. "And now you are here to find some answers?" he asked soft and humbly. I nodded again. He turned around without another word and walk out the doorway.

I looked back at Keyoni wondering if I should follow, and he nodded. I jogged after him.

"I don't get why this is such a problem. It seems to me that a gift like this would come in handy." I said when I slowed to a walk and followed closely behind him with Keyoni next to me.

"That, you are right about, but the things that could've come with this gift and the creature that it came from could cause a change within you. It might not be a change for the better. This gift could indeed become a curse. Not just to you but to the world." Rahmeeku responded as we reached the bottom of the steps.

"Wait…when you say creature you are still talking about a vampire right?" I asked.

Rahmeeku looked back at Keyoni noticing his aggravated worry. "You really don't remember do you, and I take it he didn't tell you." Rahmeeku said. I shot a suspicious glare back at Keyoni and he hung his head with his hands behind his back as if trying to avoid eye contact.

"The only way you can have a gift like this is by drinking the blood of a vampire. Not just any vampire though. The blood would have to come from the first. Antony is more powerful than any other vampire. He's the only one capable of sensing auras," Rahmeeku said, as he shuffled around in a book then had begun crushing and combining herbs with water.

My eyes got wide. I knew who he was talking about. I now had a name and face to the shadowy figure. His name was Antony, the first vampire…one of the six. I looked back at Keyoni with concern then walked over to him. "What are you not telling me?" I asked, suspicious of why something of this magnitude would be kept from me.

Keyoni looked at me desperately. "He's been after you for a long time. We don't know why," he said.

I stepped back "If you knew who it was then why are we here?" I asked with a frustrated tone.

Rahmeeku stepped in with an answer, "Because, I am the only one that knows how to find him. You are going to have to forgive him. He is the only other one that did know. The burden of keeping a secret like that is wearing on the mind and soul. He knew what changed in you but not how. He didn't know what to expect, therefore, he saw no reason to inform anyone unless it became an issue. Would it be easy for you to tell someone you loved so much that their soul was possibly damned? Keyoni also holds a fearful suspicion that you might have loved Antony and never truly stopped," he said. I looked down at my feet. I was feeling ashamed for misunderstanding Keyoni's intentions. Rahmeeku was right. What Keyoni was going through was harder for him than I realized. I looked back up at Keyoni with forgiving eyes and he half smiled melting my heart into my blood stream.

"You'll have to find Antony in order to find the answer. He is the only one who knows the real details of it," Rahmeeku said, as he poured the ingredients in a large bowl then spoke more, "Antony hid his steps well but not well enough. He hides in a continent unknown to most and inhabited by natives with very light brown skin. You must first go to the natives. They will know how to find the werewolves. The werewolves are your only hope of finding him. Only they know where he is and how to get there. Please, don't ask why. That's another long story. Take this talisman and a vile of blessed honey water. When you reach the unknown continent drink the water it will hide your scent from the werewolves," Rahmeeku said.

"Why would they want to harm me? I've done nothing to them," I asked.

"Because like mankind there are good ones and there are bad ones. The bad ones will be waiting for you. Now you must go," Rahmeeku said. We said our good-byes then Keyoni and I made our way back to the underground. Michael and Keyoni arranged for a ship to take us; Lee, me, and two others, Silus and Tyron, to the unknown continent.

Silus and Tyron are new guys I just met but old friends to Keyoni. They too are immortal, but I still had quite a few thousand years on them. They were also brothers…and shape shifters. Their parents were mixed perfectly of all the blood lines of the first six. Their skin was dark like Rahmeeku's and that of an African warrior ran thick in their blood but also a sense of honorary brotherhood. They didn't dress like African warriors, but they each had the heart of one nonetheless. After their parents died, they had to fend for themselves.

Silus was nineteen and Tyron was twenty-three. One night, they were attacked by a hungry lioness. She jumped on Tyron and started biting and lashing the more he fought back. Silus started to throw rocks and shout at her. Tyron lost consciousness and she leapt at the arm that was throwing the rocks knocking Silus to the ground. With one front paw holding down his head and the other holding down his arm, she began gnawing on the flesh of his arm. Silus saw Tyron's spear laying inches away from him. Silus grabbed it and speared her rib cage with one arm as she did a hefty amount of damage to the other then she limped off. Tyron had gashes all over him and was bleeding heavily. Keyoni was in flight and saw the fight. Impressed by their bonding strength, he took them to Rahmeeku. They have been Keyoni's devoted friends ever since.

Lee, Michael, Silus, Tyron, and I traveled by horse while Keyoni flew just above the clouds with protectively watchful eyes on us. By now it was mid-December and a light fall of snow began. I had on the outfit Lee had made for me, thick black wool gloves lined with cotton insulated black silk and a, curve complimenting fit, long and thick dark grey coat with thick cotton insulated dark lilac colored silk lining the inside. The hood and sleeves were wide and bordered around about three inches wide with black silk rope that twisted, curled and curved like grape vines without the grapes or leaves. Lee wore a coat of the same design but it was light brown with dark brown rope and the silk lining was forest green.

We stayed mainly in the forest off the path. As we rode I could hear Silus and Tryon whispering back and forth to each other. Silus rode up next to me. "How are you?" he asked smoothly.

"I'm doing well," I said grinning without meeting his stare.

"I was thinking—"

"Silus don't do it," Michael said as he came up on the other side of me. Silus didn't break the holding stare that scaled me causing him to not notice what was coming up ahead.

"If you are ever looking for a new bodyguard then please let me know because I would love to guard you're—" *Smack!* His face smooshed against a big tree branch that was hanging low and he was knocked off of his horse as I ducked my head. Michael, Lee, and I rode on laughing lightly. Silus's horse stopped about a foot ahead then the branch disappeared and Keyoni came from behind the tree smiling with the look of satisfaction in his eyes. He tossed the branch aside then leaned forward and helped Silus up. Tyron rode by slowly laughing a good, deep and hardy laugh while Silus glared at him.

Silus then looked at Keyoni, "Sorry. I uh...wasn't thinking right... you know what I mean?" Silus said.

Keyoni smiled again then said, "It's okay. You got set up and hey... you got an eternity to get him back." Then he disappeared behind the clouds again in an instant. Silus smiled then snickered happily. He then got back on his horse and caught up with the rest of us.

Big yet beautiful shimmering white puffy flakes of snow met us at the pier along with the captain. The ship was immaculately beautiful. The wood was Greek and Italian. On the railing, it looked like wood had grown like rope and twisted its way around like it was outlining the ship. There were carvings all over it in a Latin language to either keep something in or out. Maybe both. The bow was carved into an angel on one half and a frightful demon on the other half. The sails were black and thick like tar. The captain was as silent as a graveyard and as mysterious as blank headstones. Never speaking a word and cloaked in darkness, he hid his face well.

We shipped off after dark in a thick blanket of snow to hide us well. I learned some new games, had a few drinks, Keyoni taught me how to ballroom dance better, Lee's tranquil voice sang a song and we all laughed at Silus's comical theatrics. I got a chance to know everyone more. With all they have been through in their lives they were still very happy and reasonably optimistic. Keyoni and Lee picked at each other off and on throwing some of their arsenal my way and Michael told more about his journeys. Watching them gave me another reminder of what I was going through all this for. The love, good humor, and happiness were bright and very alive that night. The love of friends and family are always worth it.

When it got late and we all decided that we had enough to drink, everyone headed off to bed. As tired as I was...all I could do was toss and turn for four hours. By then I had sobered up. Needing some fresh air, I decided to get up and come on deck. I passed by the captain who didn't flinch or turn his head in my direction once. He kept both hands on the wheel with his head pointed directly forward, his hood still casting a dark shadow over his face.

I leaned over the bow and watched it push through the mighty ocean like a quiet stampede making way through curtains. The snow had been left behind and the clouds with it. We had gone further that I realized. The reflection of the night sky and the glorious shinning stars made the water seem black with diamonds floating in it like feathers. They glistened with every small ripple. It was the most peaceful moment I had in a long time. The air brushed lightly against my cheeks and danced with strands of my hair. I closed my eyes and directed my head toward the sky to take in the peace of mind.

I could feel a presence behind me. I popped my eyes open and turned around startled. The captain was standing right behind me idly holding a stick with a lantern hanging from it his sleeve covering the hand that held the long bamboo stick. I peered a little trying to see his face, but I still couldn't make a face for him underneath his dark hood. He held out his other hand as human as any other and a little dirty. I slowly reached my hand toward his pausing for only a second out of hesitation. When our hands touched it felt like a bolt of lightning shot through my body and I was in a trance. It seemed as though my soul was traveling. I came to a place that was devoured in a white light. Out of the light came a figure as it got closer I could see a man with a pleasantly calm and somewhat familiar face. His hair was sleek and dark brown with tight curls that hung to his jaw line. His brown eyes sparkled. They were like morning dew on a tree trunk.

He stopped just two feet in front of me and smiled contently. I stared in confusion. "You look just like your mother," he said.

My eyes got wide, "You knew my mother?"

"Correction, I know your mother. You and Michael have made us both so proud," the man said.

I creased my eyebrows in disbelief and still confused, "Who are you?" I asked.

He smiled looking remarkably a lot like Michael and it started to come together. My eyes filled with tears as I gasped then gulped my heart back down to my chest. He cautiously stepped forward and slowly embraced me with a gentle hold. The energy that flowed from him was familiar and comforting. I wrapped my arms around his broad shoulders and buried my head in his neck, then began to cry. "Ssshhh, my child," he said in a slight whisper. I lifted my head and he gently put his hands on each side of my face. "If you couldn't do this you wouldn't be here," he said, as if he read my mind. I sucked up my emotions nodding. My father brought his hands back down to his side and spoke again, "The captain is a direct link between this world and all others. This includes heaven and hell but he can only allow so much time and mine is short so I need you to listen carefully." I nodded again lightly and kept my tears contained. "The painting that Leeana took out of the house has a message in it. It's a coded message that will give exact instructions and ingredients for the greatest weapon you'll ever need. Michael and the others know that but what they haven't figured out is how to decode it. Take it to a woman named Paelona. She'll be able to help you. Promise me something though…" I nodded. "Do not let this painting out of your sight. That much power can drive even the best to do horrible things in order to have it. Promise me."

"I promise," I said "

Good, now come here," My father hugged me tightly and I hugged him as well, "I must go now. Your mother sends her deepest love for you and your brother as do I," he said calmly.

"Ohhhh." I sobbed. "Just a little longer? Please." I buried my head into his neck as my tears began to flow.

My father sighed mournfully holding me tighter and then said, "If it were up to me. I would still be alive and right there with you. Then you would be asking for more time away from me." I giggled under my breath. He loosened his arms and I knew I had to let go. He took a step back smiling at me then disappeared as I was sucked back into reality.

I opened my eyes with a gasp for air. I looked at the captain and he slowly slipped his hand from mine and reached underneath his robes with the other hand, which looked like shiny black bone with pieces of charred flesh on it. He pulled a sword in a plain steel sheath out of his robes. He slowly unsheathed the sword then laid it in my hands. The blade was three feet long, wavy and folded perfectly. The steel shinned a bright silvery light with a blue tint and the handle was darker steel welded in the shape of a dragon's head. Its dark steel thin tongue ran down the middle of the blade with leather braided on tightly in layers for better grip. At the other end of the handle was another blade about six inches long and wavy also but only half the width of the main blade. The captain carefully grabbed it then put it back in its sheath and held it out suggesting me to take it.

"It's a gift. Take it or he will feel insulted," Michael said suddenly standing a few feet behind the captain at the bottom of the steps on the main deck.

I looked at the captain, took the sword in both hands, and nodded, "Thank you…for everything," I said. He nodded underneath his hood and floated like the mist back to his wheel.

"He, luckily, believes in what you fight for. This sword is his way of providing help besides taking us to our destination. As a matter of fact, he probably made that himself," Michael said as I came down the stairs.

"What is he?" I asked.

We both leaned on the side railing of the ship. "Before he died he was a warrior unlike any other. He was also a man just like any other who had seen and done more bad than good, but when he died to save an entire village, his soul became the first that had an equal amount of good and bad in it. A perfect balance. So…as punishment for the bad things he did, the gods did what you have seen on his hands to his entire body. Half human and half demon. They ordered him to provide transportation for all beings whenever called upon. For the good that he did, they gave him their full protection and the immortality on earth that he asked for. He, like us, discovered the true power of freewill, broke free of their grasp, and now only transports who he sees fit, and well, as you know, makes it possible to talk to whomever he is willing to allow. He's also among the best of the alliances we have."

"Does he talk, ever?" I asked.

Michael grinned. "He never needs to," he answered.

"It is a little creepy," I said, looking back at the captain over my shoulder.

Michael snickered. "Yeah, I think he prefers it that way."

"What's his name?" I asked, as I kept my gaze on the captain.

"John."

I shot my head back over to Michael. "John? Really?" I said in disbelief.

Michael giggled lightly, "What were you expecting?" "I don't know. Gabriel, Arthur, or Luthor. Something more dominating or God-fearing I guess. Not John. Can he hear me?"

Michael snickered again. "Yes, but don't worry he's heard that a lot and doesn't get offended easily."

"Oh," I said, looking down at a ring on my finger that I began to spin around my finger.

"I saw our father, Michael."

Michael looked out to the horizon then said, "That doesn't surprise me. John is the only one that knows how to find him. He hid him and the parents that started the existence of your soul. Not to mention, he's the only one that can do such things. He strongly disagreed with what the gods did to your parents. He refused to believe that any creature or being should be punished for loving another. He thinks it's a good thing knowing that demons are capable of love." I looked down to the water watching the lights from the dimly lit lanterns on the ship prance along the water.

"How old is he?" I asked

"He got 4,323 years, 2 months, 5 days, 3 hours, and twenty-two seconds on you," Lee said walking toward us. She then leaned on the rail on the other side of Michael.

I lifted my eyebrows and widened my eyes briefly while I said *wow*, and Michael smiled then looked at her. It was nice to see that Michael was loved so much. Every time they looked at each other their passionate love would radiate around them.

Keyoni was suddenly next to me and I jumped a little. "John knows you better than you ever will." he said.

I slapped his arm. "Stop doing that!" I said.

Keyoni grinned making me feel warm inside. My heart was fluttering but I tried to play it off by rolling my eyes, then I turned to find Michael and Lee gone. "They do that sometimes," Keyoni said.

I turned my head back to him then said, "Well at least they don't do it as much as you do." I grinned.

Keyoni's eyes lit up, "Wait was that…yes, I do believe that was a joke," he said smiling. Taken in, yet again, by his smile…my grin turned into a smile as I kept leaning on the railing.

"How is it that you guys know him and I don't?" I asked.

Keyoni leaned his back against the railing then looked at me. "You've heard the stories about the boat man that ferries the dead to the underworld right?" he asked. I creased my forehead and my eyebrows dipped in slightly.

"Yeah, I also heard it was a myth."

"Only some of it, but you can easily figure that one out. You don't find him…he finds you. He prefers it that way. John came to Michael when you were born. John told Michael he couldn't let him die because his existence was important for your survival. But that's all he told him. Your mom was told the rest in the premonition she had earlier. He kept a close eye on Michael making sure that Michael kept away the evil long enough for you to grow up then John came to us all when Michael found Lee and I. He told us what was gonna happen to you and offered to help. Said he was waiting for me to find Michael and eventually caused the crossing of our paths. My sister and I only found you in three of your human lives. I guess the timing and events to come just weren't right for him until now," Keyoni said.

I nodded my head a couple times slowly then looked down at my ring and fiddled with it some more. "You know…even the gods need rest. This is the Dark Ages, and it seems as though they are on vacation."

I snickered lightly, then sighed and said, "I guess somebody has to take care of things here while they're gone." I turned my head to look at him, "Come get some rest; we'll worry about the painting tomorrow,"

Keyoni said stepping off of the railing and holding out his hand for mine. I curved my eyebrows in ward a little in confusion. "Yeah, I can read minds remember. Sorry but I had to know what was bothering you," he said. I grinned and took his hand. I should have remembered that. I know better and now Keyoni knows that I was fidgeting with my ring was because I was becoming sexually frustrated every time he is near. This time though, I didn't stop myself from thinking about it. He wrapped one arm around me as we walked toward the steps that went below.

"Don't even think about it. You're not getting in there yet."

"What?" he said sarcastically.

"I can read minds too…remember," I said. Keyoni chuckled quietly and short then kissed my head and we went to bed. I made him sleep in his own space.

The dreams that I had been having my whole life were becoming more vivid and terrifying. Even though I slept…it was not a peaceful rest. The beasts that we fought were of all kinds mythical and not. The world around us was a lot different than anything I had ever seen. What I now know were cars lay abandoned all around rusting away and falling apart. Tall buildings that use to reach for the sky were abandoned, burnt half way down, or demolished and laid in a ruble beneath our feet as we battled creature and human alike. There were hybrids. Part human and part something else. Blood and chaos was everywhere.

We were all fighting the evil and I had just made another kill then notice the sun breaking through the black smoke-filled clouds. I looked up to the sky and everything began to fade. I knew I was waking and closed my eyes to take in the sun.

I could feel the warmth of the sun brushing along my cheek. I woke to see the sun gently peering in the small window of the ship as if saying good morning. I slowly sat up, stretched, then stood and notice that I had nothing cover my bottom but an over sized blouse that almost touched my knees. I sighed heavily and rolled my eyes then directed my head over to the door of my sleeping quarters. I could hear the others talking and laughing amongst each other which was nice. I grinned widely then walked over and opened the door.

"Good morning, beautiful," Keyoni said sitting at a wooden table with benches. Michael, Silus and Tyron were sitting with him and lee was serving food and drink to the hungry men. The guys all looked at me smiling. Michael nodded with a mouthful. Tyron was sitting next to him and waved as he took a drink. Silus and Keyoni were sitting across from them.

Silus took a quick drink. "Wow! A woman that still looks good in the morning. You're a lucky man," he said nudging Keyoni.

I smiled then raised my eyebrows and set my hands on my hips and said, "He hasn't been that lucky and won't be if he's not a good boy." I looked over at him playfully.

"Oooohhh!" Tyron blurted out in a giggle and the rest of them laughed lightly.

Keyoni smiled heavenly. "I'm always good."

"You hungry, hun?" Lee asked. I looked at her and nodded. Keyoni and Silus scooted over to make room for me as I walked over to the table. I sat at the end of the bench next to Keyoni and he pulled my head close to kiss the side of my head.

There was fresh Italian bread on the table and Lee set glasses of cold milk and fresh orange juice in front of me along with a plate of fried eggs, ham, mixed fruit, a stack of three medium-size buttered pancakes topped with pecans, and a small jar of pecan syrup and on the side. Too hungry to care enough, I didn't bother to ask how she did it, on a ship too. We chatted about good memories of the past laughing and picking on each other a little. When we finished eating we talked about uncovering the code on the back of the painting after we all got dressed.

I went to my quarters and pondered over what I would wear. It seemed that nothing exciting would be happening and there's no special occasion there for I decided to go with comfort. I put on a white cotton peasant blouse that hung down showing my shoulders with a black ribbon that I tied to tighten just above my breast line. The sleeves were puffy. I tucked the bottom of the blouse in under the waist line of a deep red long skirt I put on then stepped in my boots.

As I bent forward to secure my boots something came bouncing to my attention. "I do remember something from the life that was dazzled from my memory. Oh my god!" I whispered under my breath. I covered my mouth; my eyes were wide open with shock. This is not good...definitely not good! Why couldn't I remember this before? I thought to myself. I scurried up off the bed and ran out the door. I banged on all the doors in search of Lee; she wasn't in her quarters. After pounding on the door and coming into yet another empty room…I closed the door and turned to continue my search heading up to the deck. I began to trot up stairs then stopped myself suddenly as I reached for the doors.

A soft voice spoke from behind me, "Your right. Keyoni doesn't know now and doesn't need to know just yet," Lee said. I whipped my head around my eyes wide with astonishment and slight embarrassment. I knew that Lee heard my thoughts. They were practically screaming at her. I slowly came back down the steps and stood in front of her.

My head drooped down and eyes squinted "There is only one way I can do this." I looked back up at Lee. She calmly, with a sense of sympathy, looked at me.

"I know. We'll make arrangements with John. He's the only one that can help you right now, but he will only be able to hide you from Keyoni for a short time. After that I won't be able to stop him. You will have to move and think quickly if you want to find Antony before he does," Lee said. I knew what she meant. Keyoni had become overly protective due to the many years of searching for the life that would allow him to be more than just a small part of mine.

I kept my mind as blank as possible in case Keyoni snuck in. I changed back into the leather outfit from Lee and packed a few things then put on my coat. My stomach turned and knotted as the hands of anxiety crawled up my spine. I had no idea to where I would be going or if I could find Antony on time.

Something puzzled me though and I couldn't figure out what it was. I couldn't shake the feeling that something was missing from this equation. There was something that they were keeping from me but what and why is this one the only life that I had to drink an elixir to remember my souls past? According to my new developed memory I never needed any help remembering who I really am. Then again maybe they don't know. Rahmeeku did say that I would have to find Antony if I wanted to find the truth. He just didn't specify how much truth I would find.

I finished packing, threw the bag over my shoulder and picked up my staff then turned and came to a halt covering my mouth to conceal my deep gasp. Lee and John were both standing close behind me. Lee handed me a satchel of food and water. "Just hold onto him and close your eyes. Don't ask any questions. Even I don't know where you're going. Anything you need to know John will tell you; there will be no need to ask. Remember to steady your thoughts and focus on what you need to do nothing else. John can only hide your trail for one night and two days. John said that one of those days would be spent on getting you to the destination. So your time will be short," Lee said. I nodded assuringly and she swiftly made her way out to keep the guys distracted, which was not hard.

I wrapped my arms around John's torso and dug my face into his chest squeezing my eyes shut as tightly as possible. Just as soon as I did so it felt as if I was the fog from dry ice being dropped in salt water. Crawling quickly over the ocean to land and I could no longer feel him. Suddenly we came to a stop. I landed on one knee softly and I could feel the ground beneath me and smell the cold but sweet fresh night air with the calming sent of pine.

I opened my eyes and looked around. I was in a small clearing and John was gone. Moonlight showed bright through the broken up clouds. The ground was covered with thick powder like snow that sparkled like finely ground glitter. Small patches of grass grew tall and shimmered green. Evergreens of all kinds encircled the clearing unevenly cradling the beautiful snow on their branches. A freezing breeze swept through chilling the bones in my hands. I bent down putting a bag in front of me on the ground and then squatted down. I pulled my gloves out of a side pocket on my bag and slid one on. As I slid the other one on I heard the snap of a twig come from the woods just ahead as if something was lurking. Taking advantage of the darkness and hiding in the shadows that the thick trees provided. I kept my head in that direction and froze landscaping my eyes on the woods.

As slow as molasses in this cold air, I unsheathed my sword from my back. I locked my grip on it remembering that I had not drunk the blessed honey water yet. If the wolves were her they could definitely smell me. I brought the sword to my side then slowly stood. I saw two bright blue eyes illuminating like crystals shown in the dark holding an eerie glare at me. It stepped into the moonlight and I got a good view of what I was dealing with. It was a wolf. His hair was like thin strands of silk that glistened with a silvery tint. His head was as big as the top half of my body. He could've swallowed my head whole in one bite. That was very clear to me.

He took a couple steps toward me then stood on its hind legs to show his massive muscles. It was six feet tall with a torso shaped like a man who was as wide as two of me. He was standing proud like a man and I got the point. He was a werewolf. A werewolf with intent on killing me; At least that's the feeling I got when he lowered his head with his glare still fixed on me and let out a deep growl showing his fangs to add to the ferociousness of his nature. Then he huffed and breathed in heavily then shot his head toward the moon and howled. His body was arched back and his chest puffed out. It was a beautiful harmonious sound yet, dangerous.

My heart raced and though it was freezing, my palms began to sweat. I steadied my breathing and focused on him still. My hand squeezed the handle of my sword even tighter. He dropped down on all fours and after the snapping of more twigs out of the dark came four more about his size. I quickly scaled my situation then continued my focus on their fearless leader. The other four were not as immaculate but big nonetheless. He grinned slightly and I returned a bigger grin. "Five? That's just insulting," I said in a sarcastic tone. I could feel natural instincts that I wasn't aware of before all this. It made me confident. Although getting out of this alive did seem almost impossible.

The other four inched in slowly swaying slightly from side to side. They held a stare and low growl as they came closer. Their leader snapped at them and they hesitated. He was telling them to wait. But why? I creased my eyebrows inward, eyeing him with a suspiciously confused look. He stood on his hind legs again. Smoke began to secrete from him. His thick fur turned to ash and floated to the ground. He squinted then began to huff and puff before howling at the moon in agony of the pain as his flesh began to char and blacken.

I started feeling sorry for the beast. I grit my teeth then pursed my lips together. I had no idea what was happening. 'Is he dying? Is this a trick? Focus...focus.' My mind was having a little bit of hard time getting a grasp on what was happening. That was the question... *What* was happening? My grip stayed strong on my sword.

His howl turned into the cries of a man then he calmed with his eyes still squinted shut. A small breeze swept through. His flesh turned to ashes and danced away to reveal a man. He was gorgeous. He had long red wavy hair, dazzling blue eyes, and still six feet tall. But his build was surprisingly average and nowhere near as muscle bound as the wolf form. He slowed his breathing and opened his eyes. He looked at me as an unsettling grin formed. I shot a glance at the other four then looked back to him.

"Don't worry, lass. They won't move...yet," he said releasing a smile. I scoffed at him. "So...you're the one?" he said mockingly "My name's David. Aye, yer much prettier than the last life. T'would be a shame to mangle a face like that...again." He smiled when I twitched my head in confusion. "Now, what would you be doin here by yourself now?" I looked at David smugly because I realized his Scottish accent.

I decided to answer his question with another question, "What's a European werewolf doing so far from home?" I asked.

"We have clans all over the world. Not sure where you'd pop up. Who would've guessed that you would land thirty-feet away from me."

Why did John put me here? So close to danger. I thought to myself. I wondered if John really was the alliance we thought he was. It seemed that he was trying to get me killed. "You must have a lot of patience. It has been a while since I was last here," I said pretending to remember.

David smiled with a glare that sent stinging chills up and down my spine. "Not patience, my dear. All out of that. It's more like... determination. Mostly to piss off my sister. She doesn't agree with our little campaign. Sibling rivalry...I'm sure you know," he said.

I mildly shook my head a couple times then said, "Not really."

David snickered. "Like I said, no patience, dear. We've wasted enough time," he said then stood stiff and began to huff and puff. David was taking his wolf form again and I readied myself.

After his horrifying transformation, David dropped with a thud to all fours and growled in his chest with his head lowered. His eyes glared at me intensively. David began to cautiously move toward me. I took a fighting stance. My feet in place and my grip still fastened to the handle of my sword. Focus, focus, focus. I calmly coached myself. I measured my enemies. I kept a cautious eye on all of them.

One of the four with sleek red hair leaped at me from my right side. I quickly spun around clockwise slashing his side open. Another slammed into my back knocking me to the ground. I held my face up and reached behind me grasping onto oversized handfuls of fur and threw him of me. He flew ten feet and slammed into a tree so hard that pieces of bark spouted off. I was impressed my newfound strength which seemed to come so naturally. The two wolves whimpered and limped away.

The woods creaked and moaned as something else moved through it from a short distance. I hopped on my feet and spun around to block an attack. The other two each latched on an arm taking me down to the cold frozen ground again. Then David approached and held me down with his paws. One paw was on my shoulder to keep me from struggling too much. I screamed like a wild banshee as they dug into my flesh with their teeth and razor sharp claws. David slowly stepped onto my body and I thought I heard a laugh grumble from his belly. I cockily spit in his face. David shook his head then swiped at my side. The squishing sound of ripping flesh and the detrimental pain was unbearable. I screamed loud enough that that the wolves whined slightly at the screeching in their ears.

Then from the shadows came a howling unlike another. It was almost heavenly but a little sharp toned as if to give warning or a scolding. David and the other two shot a glare at the trees ten-feet ahead of them.

The creaking and moaning of the woods were closer now. I could hear swooshing in the trees. *Swoosh...Swoosh...Swoosh.* I could feel the ground thudding and make out the sound of running horses. Then, out of the shadows emerged another wolf. From where I was I could see that the wolf was female. She had white hair that shined as if the gods had colored her with the glistening light of the stars and breathe taking green eyes. Her build was much larger and firmer looking than David's but also feminine. David glared at her then let out a low growl.

She returned a more vicious growl. As I lay underneath him my blood drained steadily from my left side. I could feel consciousness slowly slipping away from me.

The other two wolves loosened their claws in me and each shot their glare to the trees about six feet to the side of them as the crunching of leaves and twigs surrounded us. The swooshing got louder. Flashes of more than one thing zigzagging through the trees seemed to be a threat to the wolves for I could detect a hint of furious concern for themselves.

David and the female wolf leapt at each other locking their jaws on each other's throats, ripping and scratching at each other as they gnawed on one another. They snipped and snarled violently throwing each other around. They rolled all over each other. Blood and drool spattered into the snow. Meanwhile in a quick blur the other two wolves were blindsided by something or someone that moved to fast to be seen. The two wolves seemed to be fighting with blurs and they were losing just as I was losing the fight with consciousness. My vision was that of a drunken person working on little to no sleep. My eyes could only flutter subtly. The sound of the miniature battle faded into a muffle and my lungs were no longer willing to do much more than very lightly breathe.

Suddenly there was silence. The silhouette of a man with long black hair knelt at my side. A nervous tension sprang up my body allowing enough coherencies to give me slight strength. I griped my sword that still lay in my hand and barely lifted my arm. The man gently wrapped his hand around my wrist without squeezing and effortlessly pushed it back down. His gentleness gave me a hint that he was there to help. Good thing too cause that little bit was all I had left. What choice did I have? I was bleeding to death. The man lifted me in his arms and I passed out.

A New Discovery

When I started to wake I could feel the warmth and hear the soft crackling of a fire. The smell of fresh jasmine filled the air. I slowly opened my eyes to see a beautiful woman sitting at my bedside who seemed oddly familiar. She had curly flowing firry red hair and sapphire glowing green eyes. Her skin was so fair and pale, like David's. Even the features of her face complimented her exotically shaped body that was well accented in a deep green gown. It was thick and covered her back and shoulders with a big thick hood. The gown was held together with ribbon that crisscrossed from the middle of her cleavage to the bottom of her mid drift where it was sown together perfectly and flowed liked a mini green pond on the ground. Her sleeves were long and very wide at the end. The wrist end of the sleeve folded over and had beautiful golden

Celtic knots border lining them. Underneath she wore a very thick and tight long sleeve plain white dress that didn't cover her cleavage much.

Her smile could've calmed a raging lion. She put her dainty soft as silk hand on my hand, "How are ya feelin love?" she asked. Her voice was as soft as her skin.

"Okay…I think," I answered thinking to myself that could this really be David's sister? Was this the same white wolf that fought so savagely?' I suddenly realized how ok okay I really was. No pain…no pain at all. I mean, how anyone or anything could not feel pain after getting their body ripped open.

I must have not been hiding my confusion as well as I thought cause she giggled then said, "Yes it was me and don't worry yourself none. It was just herbal medicine and I must say you heal wonderfully, love." I lifted a side of the thick bear skin that covered me and nothing was there not even dry skin, just fur. I rubbed on it in disbelief. "I felt John comin. But I was not expecting you yet. John must've known that, where David is I wouldn't be far behind. Putting you there slowed him down enough for me to catch up with 'em."

My eyes popped open and I shot up, "I was used as bait!" I shouted, and then she smiled again.

"Think of like this…if I would've never caught up with him, he would have found you and the others when you got here. Someone would've been ripped to pieces before Keyoni could transform. By the way, what are ya doin here?" She got up and got water from a clay bowl with a wooden cup. I sat up and realized that I was wearing clothing that I couldn't name. A long sleeve dress, but made some kind of fabric that I hadn't seen before. Silver ribbon crisscrossed up along my spine keeping my back covered. The dress went down to my ankles and at the waist was section into four to allow more free movement. It was dark blue with silver Celtic rope design bordering the slightly widened sleeves had small ruby red, gemstones. There was a tighter long sleeve black shirt and tight black pants underneath. The shirt was made of hemp and soft. The pants were black leather.

"I made the outfit myself. Does it fit well?"

I nodded a few times. "It feels great, and it's very warm. Thank you."

She gracefully nodded once then said, "You're welcome love. Luckily for you your boots were untouched. So we saved them for you, too." She pointed over to a stump and handed me water.

I sipped the water then something dawned on me. "You still haven't told me your name." I said.

"Of course, forgive me, darlin'. The name's Myrah." She smiled proudly. I smiled back suddenly calm again. I look around in awe at the cone shaped domain I was in.

Myrah giggled. "It's a teepee love. This is Ojibwa territory. Their native to this untamed land. They're also shape shifters that believe the animals are their ancient ancestors and here to guide them. So they take the form of the animal that represents each ones personality and strength. I did not have a choice. David thought that if he changed me I would be a general for another clan. I'm not a heartless wretch though. I have answered your questions will you tell me now why you're here so soon…alone?"

I hung my head trying to think of where to start. I had no time for detail. "I need to find Antony," I said.

Myrah half smiled than looked down at her perfectly dainty hands rested on top of each other in her lap. "I thought he'd have somethin to do with it," Myrah said.

I sat up and crisscrossed my legs to face her pulling the fur blanket over my legs. "Do you know what happened?"

"I know more than I should, but, alas, I'm not sure that I'm the right one to be tellin ya." Myrah said. An old pleasant looking man with thick, straight, long, black and grey hair stepped in lightly leaning on a tall staff. He smiled warmly. His skin seemed soft and almost a caramel color. On each side of his face a section of hair had beads at the ends holding tightly an eagle feather. He had a grey and white fur cloak and his dear skin outfit was highly decorated with more beads and feathers that dangled. Some beads were sown to the fabric. Even his moccasins were decorated with intricate beadwork, which gave me the impression that he was someone important.

"Only you can explain what you saw. It was very important part of her life, and she has the right to know," the man said kindly to Myrah. She stood so gracefully and seemed to almost float to him.

Myrah gently embraced him with a hug then looked at him and said, "Aye…you're right. Pan, this is Chief Tekatin," she said I could tell his name was hard for her to push out. The name was familiar but couldn't remember why.

"You can just call me Chief. She does," he said giving a quick nod in Myrah's direction. Myrah smiled playfully cocking her eyes to the side.

The cold nipped a little upon removing the blanket but only for a second. I stood to show respect and shake his hand. The chief smiled and shook my hand then gave me a quick measure. "I came to see why my son is gone from home so much and now I understand. You are as beautiful if not more on the inside as you are on the outside. You have been blessed with the good morals, and strength of an angel's soul, and the free spirit of a demon. Yet you are a human untainted by evil temptations. If I was him I would be just as devoted," the chief said with such soft words it gave me chills and shocked me. It was if he could see right into my soul…my mind. This no doubt must have been his gift and the reason he was chief.

Suddenly, I remembered why his name was familiar. He was…no, is Keyoni's father. Keyoni was found amongst the wreckage of a ship at the tender age of five. He was the only survivor in the dead of a very harsh winter even the probability of that was slim to none. To them fate had spoken. I only met him once briefly before Keyoni became a dragon. We had to get the okay from the chief before going through with it. So it's been a while. Hence, the reason for lack of memory.

"You're Keyoni's father. If you don't mind me asking…how are you still alive?" I asked.

The chief gestured for me to sit back down then sat where Myrah was seated next to my bed. "The Ojibwa have had their own ways of majick since time began. But only the chief is allowed immortality. When he left to explore the world I knew it was only a matter of time before he would find true love. I am free to die when I pass it on to my successor. Who has yet to come home, but I bear no ill will. I am a patient man and so are his people. We have accepted that his return may not be for many hundred years to come," The chief explained. I half smiled. "I will go and let you get ready while Myrah helps you put together some of the pieces of your past. When you are ready someone will bring you your belongings and some gifts from the tribe for your journey. They believe in you as do I," the chief said.

He then stood and bent forward. He lightly kissed my forehead and slowly dissipated. I looked at Myrah. "Don't worry yourself none. He prefers to travel that way," she said. I stood up and began to get my boots on.

Myrah had begun to straighten the bed. "I know that's not the explanation you wanted. All I can tell you about your last life is how you died and...what Antony's part in it is."

"I'm listening," I said, trying to get the boots on. Myrah gently grabbed the boots and I sat down on a stump.

"It was 1132 AD," she began, "you were twenty-six years old and lived in England with...Antony," she finished tying and buckling the boots then stood to see me looking at her wide eyed. Myrah sighed then stood behind me parted my hair and began braiding one side. "David found you easily over there. When you were sixteen, David and his pack of rabid pups killed your entire family. He almost killed you then, but Antony had friends too. He saved you and you fell in love with him. Because of his hazing, you never remembered who you really were and Keyoni couldn't find you." Myrah could hear my breathing quicken. I did not like where this might be going. Anxiety was beginning to rush through me like a tsunami. Myrah finished the braid on one side and got me some more water then continued on as she started braiding the other side.

"David kept a close watch but stayed out of Antony's radar. When you were three months shy of your twenty-seventh birthday..."

I inhaled deeply thinking of the one memory I had on the ship. "A face. I recognized someone enough to bring it all back. I wasn't in love with Antony...I was being held captive and I knew why as soon as my memory came back. He was keeping from someone. Someone I wanted to protect from him. I can still see her face; but this time, I don't remember who she is," I said then hung my head and continued, "Unfortunately, the memory was all that came back. I was defenseless. It's hazy but I the last image that comes to mind is me and Antony facing off. Anything more than what I just said is just too blurred," I explained.

I lifted my head back up. Myrah braided on, "All I know is that he won that fight. You were bit more than once. But then you changed. The whole universe was in an uproar. Hell took advantage of this and the Dark Ages got darker as the months went by. Even this continent was being tortured. Vikings took an evil rampage on these people along with many others. When you changed you became more and more like Antony; forgot your reason for the fight but still being protective. We don't know who either. Soon though he got an idea that came too late. He moved you guys to vamp central hoping that it would steer my soulless bastard of a brother away from his goal, but...Antony didn't realize how impatient and stubborn David was."

Myrah then paused. I'm sure she didn't hate him. After all, he was her brother. She shook her head lightly and took a deep breath then went on with the story, "David couldn't wait any longer and was willing to take his chances. David had a few of his pups attack one night. While Antony and the others that were on guard were distracted by the small battle David snuck in. Antony sensed you were in danger and who was endangering you, but he came too late to save you. Though, he was able to save his infant daughter." My jaw dropped.

Myrah finished the last braid, got in front of me, and smiled peacefully then closed my jaw and pulled the other seat close to sit in front of me. "Relax. You are not the mother. No one knows who she is. Just listen...Antony then came here knowing that me and the first werewolf were the only ones David wouldn't try...too hard, to get past. It wasn't easy for Antony to talk us in to taken the child. You see love we have an extensive past of disagreements with Antony. David followed but kept his distance and hoped that you would show up here looking for something or someone. So he stayed. Unfortunately for him he was right."

Myrah was grinning and I laughed a little then she continued, "I raised his daughter alone until the Ojibwa hunting party found us. They had been following David. He massacred two children while looking for us. They caught up with him and his pups. We heard the fight while picking berries. Her name was Adrianna. She was strong and brilliant with a fierce temper. Naturally she wanted a piece of the action and ran past me. I called to'er and they all stopped to turn n' look. Then the scared little pups disappeared. The warriors approached me and brought me to Keyoni's father who accepted us with open arms. After that Antony returned and Adrianna went to go live with her father in Persia. I don't know anymore after that or why Antony came back here now." Myrah looked at me blankly as I stared wide-eyed and in depth at the ground with growing irritation. I was a part of him at one point. Could it be true that I still was in a way?

I tried to control my breathing but I could feel anger like I have never known climbing up my body and digging into my bones. I creased my eyebrows in tightly and peered intensely at the ground pursing my lips together. "How could Antony make me forget something like this and why can't I remember everything now?" I said in a low aggravated tone as I grit my teeth together.

"You'll have to get that answer from him, love." Myrah said standing up. She flipped her hood over her head and held out her hand to me smiling again. Her beautifully angelic smile soothed me. I took a deep breath, flipped my hood up as well then took her hand and stood up. Myrah pushed aside the fabric that covered the doorway and held it open then gestured with her hand for me to go first.

I stepped out and the snow lightly crunched beneath my feet. I looked down admirably when I noticed how warm my feet still were. Keyoni did well on these. I didn't want to think of him but I couldn't help it. He knew what I was and didn't tell me. Didn't even try. I looked back up and noticed quite a few people standing around me all holding something. Myrah leaned in and whispered, "They know more about you than you realize, love. They're on your side."

A beautiful young man with medium-long, dark-brown braided hair stepped up to me. "My name is Nivoku. I'm Keyoni's much younger and cuter brother. I'm the one that picked you up. I wrapped what was left of your odd clothing around your sword then wrapped it and some food in two layers of bear skin. It's been tide tightly with our strongest hemp rope. Lucky for you, Keyoni has shown us how to make coats like yours." Nivoku set down the package of my belongings and a bedazzling young woman handed me my coat.

"I fixed it myself. I thickened the lining with tightly woven hemp and I added some fur. The winters are harsh here," she said. The woman's voice was so proud and her smile so peacefully confident.

I smiled back and said, "Thank you."

"This is my wife. Paelona," Nivoku said wrapping one arm around her lower back and kissing her temple. She smiled brightly. I realized she was caressing a small pooch in her stomach and I could feel more inspiration take over. I held my breath for a second remembering that was the name of the woman my father told me about. But now was not time.

Just then a small girl with pigtails came to me holding; who I'm sure was her little brother's hand. He was so small and stumbled about a little still learning how to balance himself. They were both a little pudgy but angels nonetheless. The little girl was maybe six and the boy no more than two. I squatted down. The little girl was carrying on one arm; grey fur that was folded perfectly with rope that was draped on top. She held it out. "You tie it around your legs from the ankle up to your knees and on your arms from your wrist to your elbow," she said with her dainty voice. I took the fur and she untied something around her brother's neck. It was a small satchel with beads intricately sown together to make a rose. I took the satchel and brushed my fingers along the beadwork. I looked at the both of them and the boy beamed with the innocence of a true angel.

"Thank you so much," I said to them then stood.

"Every one of us put some herbs and medicine in that satchel. You'll know what to use when you need it," Nivoku said. The others all approached me warmly with gifts of food, drink, stones, crystals, fur, other basic supplies, and handmade jewelry. The inspiration had taken over the fear within me. Fear and frustration dwindled more and more.

After the last gift was given to me everyone broke apart to go about their business. "Paelona, can I talk to you…alone?" I asked. Paelona nodded kindly and gestured her hand in the direction of a nearby hut. I grabbed the painting that Lee and I snuck into my belongings then followed her into the hut. Paelona took off her bearskin cloak and laid it over a large log by the fire.

"You have the painting," she said turning to me. I looked at her in astonishment. Paelona grinned then said. "I am not as young as I look. As a matter of fact...I'm what anyone would consider to be ancient. I know about the painting because I knew your father. He came to me looking for a very rare plant and I was hesitant until he explained his reason. That's when I found out about the painting. I'm glad to see that it made its way to you. I know you do not have time for it now, so I will keep it safe here. I have a feeling that you will be back." She covered all the basics leaving no questions.

"Thank you," I said handing her the painting. Paelona smiled and nodded then I left.

I put on my coat and the fur. After tying the last bit of fur to my right leg I stood and Myrah was standing in front of me holding my sword. "I can only get you started. From there you'll travel by memory so listen well when it's time for us to part," she said. I took my sword and fastened it to my side then we secured some more fur blankets over the supplies on an oversized sled.

We each grabbed a rope and pulled it behind us. Myrah and I walked for a couple hours. I talked about how I got here and she told me the way to Antony. Myrah came to a stop and I stopped a couple steps ahead when I noticed she wasn't walking anymore. I turned around. "This is as far as I go." Myrah said. I walked over to her and hugged her with a slight squeeze then she said, "Luck be with ya love. You take care now."

"I will," I said.

We pulled away and she smiled brightly, "Now hurry, before the pups catch up with your scent. The vile is in your coat pocket." I gave a quick nod and she disappeared. Just then I reached into my pocket and pulled out the vile that Rahmeeku had given me. I popped off the lid and tipped it in my mouth then quickly swallowed in one small gulp. I put the lid and vile back in my pocket and started to tread on. The hours seemed to be going so slow until I realized how close to dark it was getting.

My time was up. Keyoni would find me...soon. Too soon, before I found Antony. As I thought about it, though, he had some explaining to do. Out of all the secrets to keep this is one that should have been let out in the beginning and him of all people not telling me something like that. I'm pretty sure Michael knew too. They both kept it from me and Lee. Then it hit me what if this was Antony's plan? As a way to get me alone. He was in love with me but in a sick way...it became a game to him. His ego was over charged and he wanted the best of everything. When he found out that I had fallen for Keyoni; it's been a competition to him ever since. He wants to be my obsession. Either way I needed to find him if I wanted to know what he passed through to me.

I stopped stiffly in my tracks when the wind seemed to be quickly picking up. I knew it had to be Keyoni. I stepped back a couple feet and covered my face with my arms when the powdery snow began to kick up with the push of the wind. The wind suddenly stopped and I felt a small ripple in the earth. I slowly lowered my arm and I wanted to scream so badly, but he knew what I was thinking. I didn't have to scream out loud. I mean really...he already knew what I couldn't remember. How could he leave out a detail like that!

His angel-like eyes watered and shot small spears of plea through to my soul. My dark angel in a winter wonderland. All I could do was asked *why* in a soft yet whinny tone as I choked back my own tears.

Keyoni held back. "Antony found a way to disrupt your cause and bring more hell on earth. When he bit you and you changed; your soul suffered loudly. When you died it was in limbo where souls are randomly sorted back into human existence. You were born into a horrible family tainting your mind and morals, which made it easier for you to fall in love with him and his dark majick. You weren't you anymore. So I lost track of you. Antony was thrilled but knew it would be dangerous. He just really underestimated David. Since you had not yet committed any true crime it was possible for you to be reborn. I knew you were in Europe. I just couldn't tell where. Until—"

"Michael found Lee. Why didn't you tell me all this from the start!" I interrupted confused and frustrated trying to keep focus on the subject.

As quick as a flash of lightning Keyoni was right in front of me, almost in my face. The look in his glorious eyes was glazed with pain and a tear danced slowly down his cheek. "I had to watch you kill innocent people after he changed you the second time. I tried to find a way but I couldn't save them…or you. You cannot begin to imagine how hard that was. Before all that took place you were faithfully at my side! With him…you wouldn't even think of me!" He didn't raise his voice but grit his teeth and almost seemed to be growling lightly behind his voice. "After six hundred years of searching; I finally had you, then he took you from me…in more ways than one! I knew you would go to Antony wanting answers and," Keyoni hung his head and squinted to release more tears that blurred his vision then scoffed. He jerked his head back in my direction and intensely stared into my soul then said, "I won't lose you again. That's a risk I will not take," he said sternly. The desperation and vulnerability I saw in him was unbearable.

There was nothing I could say to that. I almost forgot what Rahmeeku said about Keyoni's fear. But it wasn't the only thing he feared with Antony. That became obvious. I found it strangely romantic for him to make such a fuss over me. I grinned playfully. "Did you really just growl at me?" He exhaled and loosened up then grinned back. I gazed into his eyes losing myself in him then carefully wiped away a tear with my thumb and embraced him stunningly in a kiss. I had no idea that I was capable of such seduction, but damn it felt good.

Surprised by my reaction he inhaled deeply then slowly exhaled as he wrapped both arms around me as I squeezed my arms around his neck to press my body against his even more. I engulfed him with my passion, and he engulfed me with his body heat. I felt like we were submerged in boiling water but didn't care at the moment. We stumbled a little backing me into a tree trunk but kept teasing each other's lips with soft kisses. Keyoni then just barely moved down to my neck and began brushing soft kisses on my neck. I exhaled lightly and slowly in ecstasy then dipped my head to the side so that he could have more room. His neck was also exposed and very close. I slowly closed my eyes. Oooohhh god! Why can I smell his sweet, pure, and undoubtedly warm blood? I thought to myself and my eyes popped open Wait, why do I want it! Shit! My eyes got wider and I inhaled deep then pushed Keyoni back with more force than I intended on or even knew I had. He looked at me innocently confused and surprised. I looked away ashamed. Something was wrong with my eyes I could feel it. I looked down at the glittering snow on the ground hoping he didn't notice that I was about to tare a hole in his neck. Something in me was willing to try although I was no match for him.

I wanted his blood more than I have ever wanted anything. The smell was explainably exciting to me and I could think of nothing to compare it to. I squinted my eyes shut still trying to avoid eye contact and gain some composure. I slowed down my rapid breathing to slow down my fluttering heart. I could still feel the intoxication of the thirst for his potent blood. Keyoni, fearlessly unoffended, came to me again and putting one finger under my chin directed my gaze back at him to see my eerie iridescent purple eyes. I looked at him desperately then said, "What's happening to me?"

Keyoni smiled chasing away every bad feeling I had. "You need to find Antony. But we have to leave now and move fast," he said. A soothing chill ran through my body when he spoke and my eyes went back to normal.

Against Time

"How 'bout another companion on your quest?" a voice said from the shadows behind Keyoni. I popped my head to the side looking around Keyoni. I knew that voice. He stepped out of the shadows and came into my sight.

A smile quickly lit up my face Keyoni turned and I shot past him, "Able!" I called. Able was the first Lycan. Young and wild. He was eighteen when he changed. Able was not very big but then again he didn't need to be. He was Irish with curly brown hair and a body that wasn't much compared to Keyoni's but it was perfectly fit for him. I choose him because of his oddly intelligent mind and his charismatic personality. Able was and still seems to be full of life. His light green eyes were full of glee. I threw my arms around his neck.

Able squeezed back. “Ey there, gurly,” he said as he spun me around once set me back down on my feet. Keyoni was already standing there glaring. They smiled at each other mischievously then in a blurry flash. Able slammed Keyoni into the snow. Able got up and stood over him. He bent over holding out his hand. Keyoni smiled.

“You still got it,” he said. Able made a couple of clicks through his teeth and winked then helped Keyoni up.

“How have you been?” Keyoni asked Able.

“Aye, the world’s been harsh, but I stay on top,” he answered optimistically. I closed one eye at him.

“How much of that did you see?” I asked knowing how nosy he can be. A sly smile stretched across his face.

“Enough. There are a couple friends of mine I’d like ya to meet.” Able said giving a quick nod at the woods behind us. A petite woman and a short but stalky man stepped out of the shadows. “That’s Elizabith but she prefers Elee. She’s from Australia and this is Hahn. He’s from Tibet. They’re hybrids. Half vampire, half Lycan, and more powerful than both. Guess you can say Antony slowly started somewhat of a new trend, darlin.”

Keyoni smiled. “Nice,” he said.

“Aye,” Able confirmed.

“We heard about you and came to offer some help. It’s what we were bred for,” Elee said spitefully taking one skip closer to me and smiled brightly.

Her smile was contagious in a funny way so, I smiled back and said, “Thank you.” Elee was small; as a matter of fact everything about her was small except for her personality, which didn’t surprise me. Able liked bouncing personalities to match his own. She stood only five feet tall but looked like the women I read about in fairytales. The front section of her flowing, perfectly curled, dark blonde, silky hair was down to her well-curved hips draping over her shoulder. Her skin was gently kissed by the sun leaving a light shade of tan with brown bright eyes that had dark and long lashes. Her lips were well shaped and plump. The color of a pink rose.

Hahn took a couple steps forward. He had muscle but was only about four or five inches taller than Eli. He was cute with medium length black hair slightly pulled back into somewhat of a ponytail and very pale skin. "If you wish for a shorter way, I can take you there. Keyoni can fly low but out of sight. Antony is more likely to be honest if he thinks Keyoni is not around. I apologize for the rush but time is short. The thirst in you is only growing stronger and you won't be able to contain it much longer," Hahn said.

My mouth popped open, "How did you know about…my thirst?" I asked.

"I am half vamp and they can sense each other. Kind of like dogs." I looked back over my shoulder at Keyoni and he nodded his head once in assurance.

I bundled up in a fur blanket then laid on the sled I was tugging with me. Keyoni kissed my forehead then laid another fur blanket on me and they tied me down loosely. I curled up and closed my eyes tight. Hahn took transformation but I kept my eyes shut. I could hear the wind howling and Hahn's paws thudding as it crunched the snow when he came down on all fours. Then there was a sudden jerk and we were off.

It seemed like it had only been a few minutes. I could hear Antony in my head. At first incoherent thoughts then full on memories and words. Hahn came to a sudden stop and untied the rope around me then helped me up. I grabbed my sword and made sure that I was still wearing the necklace Michael gave me. Hahn took my hand without a word and led me a few feet off of the trail then stopped by the trunk of a tree. Hahn then gently stood me against the tree trunk, "Wait here," he said with both hands on my shoulders. I nodded then he turned and walked a straight line into the dark.

Hahn's disappearing act made me uncomfortable. But I stayed prepared. Just then he was standing in front of me again and I gasped. Hahn quickly covered my mouth and shushed me lightly. "I was going to show you to his front door but…he knows you're here. Antony is coming to you. I have to go before he realizes that I'm with you." Hahn said then took his hand from my mouth as I nodded again. Hahn disappeared as quickly as a flash of lightning.

My head started spinning. I didn't know what to do or where to go. I looked into the darkness beyond the trees that reflected the moonlight then up to the sky that broke the clouds enough to show the moon in its beauty. "If I am being used for bait again, I'll have to kill someone." I whispered to myself.

"Used for bait huh? I bet Keyoni wasn't happy about that." It was Antony. He stood against a tree, which is three feet in front of me. He was as I remembered. Choppy-auburn colored hair that sparkled like spitting fire, pale perfectly complected skin, and light grey cold eyes. His jaw line was evenly placed and gave him that baby boy look but his body structure gave away the man in him. He was tall and fit wearing a long black coat with silver buttons on it. He wore a shirt like Keyoni's but not silk and black pants that hung loosely like the pants Keyoni wears. I figured that word spreads quickly in this world.

I glared at him. "I see you've taken to the futuristic style as well."

He smiled and said, "It's comfortable. Let's face it…I look good in anything and even better in nothing."

I rolled my eyes at the boasting of his ego then fixed my glare back on him. "What game are you playing now?" I asked crossing my arms over my chest darkening my glare at him.

"Games are for children," Antony said then in a flickering flash he was behind me. He dipped his head in and whispered in my ear.

"I do work." I spun around backing up. He was gone then suddenly right in front of me. "The thirst is getting stronger isn't it?" he asked. I said nothing as he began backing me up. "You sense the life force. You can smell it. Almost taste it." His voice was becoming seductive. My back came up against a tree. Antony put one hand above my head on the tree trunk then leaned in, "Tell me…just how bad did you want his sweet blood?" he whispered into my ear. I almost forgot that he can read thoughts and memories of the ones he had infected.

Anger flared up in my blood, and it began to boil. I breathed heavily then gave him a violent shove. Antony flipped once as he flew back about twenty feet then landed on all fours gliding to a stop. "What did you do to me?" I yelled. He shot a glare at me over his shoulder then stood and turned to face me. I started to walk toward him and he vanished again. Then like being hit with a brick wall he slammed me back into a tree.

His eyes were blood red and bright with fury. "I made you better!" He growled loudly. My anger was becoming rage and my eyes turned purple again. My muscles grew then I remembered something that would work for me. Something that dead or alive was still painful for any kind of man that had balls. In one quick shot I kneed in between his legs hard enough to lift him off of the ground a couple inches.

Antony cringed and whimpered dropping to the ground. He held onto his manhood, "Bi-i-itch," he said through his teeth tightly clinched together. I quickly got behind and stood him up with my sword at his neck.

"I've been through a lot and lied to enough. Tell me what the hell is going on and if you can't tell me how to fix it than you might wanna consider begging the gods for forgiveness because I will be sending you to them," I said with a frustrated stern voice as I pressed the sword against his throat a little more.

"Okay." Antony choked out.

I released my hold taking a couple steps back, and he slowly turned around to face me while rubbing on his neck. "Your enemies were getting desperate and you had rejected my love for far too long. They made me an offer I couldn't refuse. They offered me invincibility and a chance to get back someone I lost. So in 1013, I kidnapped you when you were only fifteen." Antony disappeared then slowly breezed by me and was behind me again. Dipping his head by my ear and speaking softly he went on. "The young age made it easier to traumatize you. Rupture the soul. You were oh so beautiful and touching your bountiful breasts was heavenly as were the few drops of blood that I trickled from your nipples. Sucking out little bits of blood at a time from different parts of your body and…"

He paused and I could hear him lick his lips then make a clicking sound. He sighed as if enjoying a childhood memory. I whipped around and he was gone again, leaving me with nothing but his voice. "Feeling you squirm, twist, turn, and arch your petite silky smooth body…Mmm…begging me to stop…pleading with me to not kill you with that angelic sobbing voice was utopia. When you screamed in pain, I had a body part of my own to stuff in your mouth. You didn't scream after the first three times I did it though. You kept your mouth shut and just filled my ears with the music of your whimpering sorrow. But between your legs..." Suddenly behind me again and quite a bit closer, he brought his lips with in inches of my neck then breathed in deeply to take in my scent. I glared intensely and my eyes watered as my temper rose like lava in a volcano then I whirled around with my sword unsheeved and Antony again, like a child playing hide and seek, was gone. A sinister low laugh echoed in the dark.

"Mmm, feeling the inside of you tremble as I penetrated you over and over was pleasure not even Aphrodite can offer. You tried so hard to push me away. You scratched and squeezed, but it only made me want it more. My favorite part though...the blood...the taste of the sweetly innocent blood that I sucked out of the plump pulsating arteries in your thighs. You took love from me so I took your innocence. Then again...you should remember. I made sure to save that memory for you." Antony then stood two feet from me and smiled a tantalizingly evil smile and his eyes went back to grey.

He was right, I could remember. It flashed before me with every word as he spoke of it. But he faded out the face of the man in my memories to protect himself. My anger washed over me like a blanket of fire. All I could think of was tearing him limb from limb. My breathing quickened but then tried to pace itself when I noticed that I could hear Keyoni's voice coming through my clouded thoughts, "If you lose control then you won't find what you came for and he wins. Focus." I heard him say. I closed my eyes, shut off my mind and took a very long deep breath. Then I opened my eyes and glared at Antony darkly.

"Continue but control your mouth." I said grudgingly. Antony held his smile then looked down to straighten his leather gloves. "Was it something I said?" he said. I growled low and he smiled bigger still looking at his gloves.

"After six years, you and your...body finally gave up and your soul was up for grabs. You see within those six years your soul had enough in it to charge an army of evil but..." Antony scoffed, "Unfortunately for me, Lucifer was the one who placed you. He grabbed you before anyone else could. Making it impossible for me to go through with the plan until I found you in the next life. Your soul was blackened enough. Though you remembered everything you were thankful to me in the next life for making you stronger. You were sick, mentally, and I wanted it. You were more than willing and ran away from home on your fifteenth birthday. That night I changed you. No one, not Lucifer or the gods expected your soul to carry some of the vampire traits with it though. But my daughter…let's just say that sometimes your precious Keyoni cares too much. He had the chance to take her out but he couldn't do it. Everyone including him knew that her being born of evil would help her become a powerful weapon. We didn't know that there were separate colonies like David's, which had their own hidden agendas to try and overrun things. Adrianna has the soul of a fallen angel reborn in human form with her mother's strength and our combined powers. She was supposed to bring about the apocalypse but not without you. You were gonna raise her as your own and show her the way. You weren't supposed to die." Antony walked over to a tree and leaned against it crossing his arms then add more.

"Lucifer disagreed and ordered Adrianna's death. I can't blame him. She became loose cannon for lack of better words. I refused, so naturally he was very unhappy with me...still is. I might be a monster but I'm not pure evil. I can't kill my own daughter and I don't hurt girls under the age of fourteen," he mockingly glanced at me in saying that and grinned slightly. I gave a warning look with a short glare. Antony snickered then continued on, "So I brought her here, played off the bad guy gone good act, so Myrah and the natives took her in. Taught her to love and be open-minded. The natives began to quickly realize how much she looked like her mother, and I knew word would reach Keyoni so I took her to Persia and hid her well I might add. He still hasn't found her…yet."

I looked at him questionably. "What?" he asked looking at me with a suspicious glare.

My eyes got wide when my brain had a sudden epiphany. "Who is her mother?" I asked. His eyes got big then he looked down to the ground and disappeared.

"Whoa. Is there something you're afraid of?"

Again all I got was his voice. "I promised her that I would never tell you and don't ask why. I hid because I don't want about it. This isn't easy sending you to kill my daughter. She is all I have left of her mother," Antony answered. I threw up my hands.

"Okay no fight this time. I'll let that one go," I said.

Antony came out of hiding right in front of me again. I put my hands down and in noticing that he spoke of Adrianna in present tense I asked, "She's still alive isn't she?" I paused and looked down in thought then looked back at Antony. "Does she know about me?"

Antony's face went blank. "No to the last question, and yes to the first. She stopped aging at twenty-five. The age you were when all of us seven began," he said, trying to avoid eye contact. I stepped to him closely and he returned my stare.

Though it was hard to contain self-control, seduction being one his many talents, I composed myself. "If she is so powerful then why am I here?"

"She's been in Persia for far too long, corrupted by war and greed. She wants to extinguish most of mankind and supernatural beings, enslave any survivors and rule a new world on earth. Mankind is not the only ones who need you." Antony sighed then hung his head. "We all do. I never considered the full harsh extent of what she could turn out to be. I just wanted to see some of mankind fall. Not her. She's the only thing I have ever truly loved aside from you and her mother. You and her mother died at the same time, but her mother was only seven months along. Adrianna would have died. Before she took her last breath I forced Adrianna's mother to drink the only blood that can give and save life." I took a few steps back realizing what he was saying. I looked down at the snow. My eyes watered and I started to feel nauseous.

I began to rub lightly on my stomach then looked up at him. "You gave her my blood. I would've been able to survive but you damn near drained me dry! Now I, Adrianna and an unidentifiable third-party member have a direct line to each other." Antony stood silent anticipating me to lunge at him.

I closed my eyes and quickly grounded myself taking a deep breath through my nose and exhaling slowly. I straightened myself back up and looked at him standing still. "Where is she and how do I get rid of this retched thirst?" I asked him with an impatient tone.

"Last time I saw her was twenty years ago in Asia. She is still in Asia, but I'm not sure where as for the thirst…" An evil smirk formed on his face and his dark eyes made me feel colder than it was.

"You're going to need blood. A lot of it. It has to be pure blood, from someone or something not of this world and yet truly good to the core. Someone like Leeana or maybe Keyoni would be so kind as to... make a donation. " His smirk turned into a smile.

I clinched the grip on my sword that I held at my side. A dragon's roar that shook the trees broke our stare. We looked up to see a black blanket shoot across the sky then came a thud that rattled the snow on the ground and allowed the trees to shed some snow off their branches. We looked back to each other. We both knew who it was. Antony smiled with so much evil you could almost imagine it oozing out of his eyes. He then said, "You don't want to kill me just yet. You're gonna need me eventually. You'll get your chance," he said then disappeared. I stood there trying to accept the truth that I found. Part of me hoped that at least some of that truth was a lie.

Keyoni and Able came out of the shadows and into the silvery moonlight with Hahn, Elee, Leeana, Michael, Tyron, and Silus. The confusion on what to do had turned into frustration and then the thirst came with aggravation. My eyes changed again and I breathed faster as I dropped to my knees. I began to rock back and forth rubbing my thigh with one hand while the other cradled my stomach. Able stopped and took a fighting stance prepared to take on his wolf form. Michael budged to rush to me but Leeana stopped him and they stood with the Tyron and Silus. Elee took fighting stance in front of them. "Oh she is really mad," Silus said watching me wide eyed with his arms crossed.

"Silus…" Tyron started in response, "You remember ten years ago, in Rome when we cornered that vampire and she almost mutilated us?"

"Yeah," Silus answered.

"Okay. She was mad. This is way beyond that." Tyron said keeping his concentration on me and Michael, in case he tried to run to me again. Silus dropped his arms still looking at me.

My body arched back with a jerk. Michael could do nothing but watch in horror as I squinted my eyes shut and tilted my head back slowly with my mouth opening wide to reveal the razor sharp fangs that grew out. Keyoni very cautiously began to approach me and Lee started after him. I shot my head in their direction. My eyes were stuck in a hungry glare while I caressed my teeth with my tongue then pursed my lips together and released an uncomforting grin. Keyoni stopped immediately as he held out his arm to stop Lee.

"Pan?" Keyoni said with weary tone though never showed even an ounce of fear or doubt.

The beast in me had awakened but not enough to come full on. Keyoni's voice had brought me back. My eyes rolled back and fluttered then I planted both hands on in the snow. I looked up at them desperately.

"Go…please," I said panting and with a desperate tone. Keyoni creased his eyebrows in and shook his head three times lightly. Suddenly the beast's anger came through. My head twitched then fixed a dark glare on him. "Why are you here?" I asked while cringing, "Answer me!" I shouted. "Do you think you can save me? Or will you take my head off with your claws? Maybe set me a blaze after tearing me limb from limb!" I screamed as the panting became more violent.

"Pan!" Keyoni said with a slightly raised tone. My head twitched again and my eyes fluttered. I came back to me and looked at both of them. My lungs were still in panic mode. Tears filled my eyes, "I don't want…" I started then my stomach felt as if someone had reached in and squeezed. Blood rushed up through my throat and out of my mouth. I got up on all fours as I gagged blood out a couple times then sat back panting a little slower. I hung my head with my arms crossed over my stomach and began to sob. My eyes still closed, I shook my head slowly "I can't. I won't." I sobbed.

Keyoni took one step to come to my side. Lee put her hand on Keyoni's chest bringing him to a halt, and he looked down to her as if pleading to not do something. She smiled a soft smile from intent to comfort Keyoni then continued to walk toward me cautiously. Lee got down on her knees in front of me and I open my eyes then slowly raised my head to look at her from behind a thin layer of hair that hung in my face. "Pan, hun," she began, "Listen to me. There is a way to help you; right now you need blood. At least enough blood that can hold off the thirst," Lee said. I could tell she was underestimating my thirst, which was why Keyoni had shown concern, but my thirst made it hard for me to be as concerned for her. Leeana exposed her neck as she leaned in to get closer to me then stopped with her neck only inches away from my mouth.

I could see her veins pulsating and smell her pure blood and as I considered it, the potent sweet aroma of someone else's blood filled the air. My iridescent purple eyes got wide with fear. I quickly stood then whispered, "No!" I shot a panicked look over at Keyoni and examined him from bottom to top. He was wearing no coat just his clothes and his sleeve was rolled up showing a very big, long, deep, and bloody cut in his left arm. The thirst raged on more and my breathing got even faster.

Lee stood up quickly. "What are you doing?" she asked in disbelief. Keyoni walked toward me with a steady pace not giving her an answer that she didn't need. Leeana slowly stepped aside.

I began to shake my head while slowly backing up, "No." I said.

"Yes. If you don't do it you will kill someone. Most likely one of them and that's something that you can never take back," he argued calmly.

"No…no!" I yelled then turned my back to him in an attempt to run.

In one motion Keyoni grabbed me from behind holding my arms to my side and dropped us both to our knees.

"Ah! No!" I screeched in a bone chilling tone. His bloody arm was wrapped around my stomach smearing blood on my coat as I wriggled to break free. He released the still bleeding arm while tightening his grip on me with the other to still hold my arms at my side.

"I won't let you run from this," Keyoni said sternly. He held out his bloody arm not even three inches from my face and clinched his fist causing fresh blood to flow out. I turned my head, squeezed my eyes shut and tried not to breath. "I can't let you kill an innocent and we both know that. You need this…trust me," he said. It wasn't him that I didn't trust…it was me. My eyes still shut. Keyoni gently kissed my neck manipulating me to naturally tilt my head toward my left putting his wounded arm pretty much on the tip of my lips and I gasped, then he whispered in my right ear. "Take it."

The smell off his blood was unbearably, spine tingling lustful. My eyes shot open and self-control was out the window. I finally gave in. I inhaled slowly relaxing my body and he loosened his grip to release my arms. My mind went into pure bliss as the sweet fume of his blood continued to linger and at that moment I forgot who he was. Everything and everyone disappeared there were no frustrating questions in my head. No fear or confusion resided in me.

I carefully gripped his forearm underhanded and kept my eyes widely fixed on his tantric blood like a hungry untamed lion cub that just caught her first kill. In giving a little squeeze for more blood flow, I raised my head, closed my eyes, and exhaled while exposing my teeth then lunged my fangs into his wound. As soon as it touched my tongue I lost my self. What most call a feeding frenzy ignited in me, and I squeezed his arm tighter, almost grinding my nails into his skin. I dug my teeth in keeping enough control to not gnaw too much harder than needed to get more blood flow. His blood was the secret to my true ecstasy. The key to my deepest, darkest, and most exotic passion. Feelings that I never thought I was capable of.

It didn't taste like blood though. It was sweet like a pineapple and burned like moonshine. If his blood was made of alcohol, then I would have been a severe alcoholic. It rippled through me rapidly like a small bolt of lightning bouncing around inside of me, awakening my soul. I could feel my body absorbing every drop like a sponge. Keyoni cringed trying to hold back the evident pain he was in as I nipped at his flesh. He gripped tighter around my waist and his body temperature sizzled. I moaned once, lightly in pleasure like an infant breastfeeding happily. After the best thirty seconds of my life, at the time, the thirst subsided. I jerked my head back up and licked my lips clean as I kept my eyes closed while savoring every last drop. Then I looked down and watched in amazement as his wound closed up then disappeared like it was never there.

I could feel myself getting back to me. I didn't feel so okay though. The shame of my actions washed over me. "You okay?" Keyoni asked softly. A look, surprised with great amazement, grew on my face and shot the look back at him. "Pure blood." He nodded.

My eyes suddenly became sympathetic. "Did it hurt?" I asked with a worried tone.

Keyoni smiled then giggled lightly and stood me up with him. I turned to him and he kept his arm around my waist as he put my hood back over my head. Still smiling like an angel of mercy he wiped off the blood on my chin with the bottom of his shirt and said, "I've defiantly had worse." Then he kissed my forehead.

I giggled under my breath then looked at him seriously. "I need to go back to the village. There's something I need to do, and it's the only safe place I have to go," I said. I wanted to get things going on figuring out the painting.

Keyoni's face went blank. I knew that Keyoni hated the thought of his father's remarks toward his destiny with his people but he exhaled slowly, hung his head and said, "Okay." He knew I was right.

On our way, Keyoni and I walked ahead with others close behind. Michael trotted up to Keyoni's other side. "Mind if I have a few minutes alone?" Michael asked rhetorically. Keyoni nodded once then we stopped and he kissed my forehead then glided back toward Leeana. I put my arm around Michaels and we continued walking.

"I'm sorry if I scared you back there," I said to Michael feeling slightly ashamed of what I became a moment ago. My eyes traced the glittering moonlight that skipped along the snow.

"Don't worry about it, Pan. I wasn't scared, just worried. I didn't want you to lose yourself." Michael hesitated then spoke again. "The reason I came to walk with you was to ask you if you really think that Keyoni could ever be persuaded to stay away from you. He had loved you for thousands of years. He fought through hell and his own purgatory all for you. Yet you still thought the evil within you, of all people, would make him walk away?" Michael said. I turned and looked at him with grief. "Back there in the woods…I could see the fear in your eyes. You were afraid that if you couldn't contain it then you would lose him forever." Michael explained.

"If I can't fix this than he will have to leave me. You don't know what that will do to him," I said.

"Not as long as he knows there is another way. I hate to make matters worse, but if you can't figure it out Keyoni will drain every last ounce of his own blood till his veins run dry. You or him? You *will* have to make that decision. I'm sorry but it is something you need to consider," Michael said stopping suddenly in front of me.

I stopped in my tracks and glared at him. I slapped both hands on his chest pushing him back a little. "Wh…" I scoffed. "How could you say that to me! Now? Right now?" I shouted grudgingly then stormed ahead of him as I felt the stress boil to the top of my head.

"Pan, I…" Michael started after me but Lee gently put one hand on his shoulder and he stopped turning his head to look at her.

"Let her go. She needs to calm herself," Lee said. Michael looked after me worried again. Lee stood in front of him and gently put her hand on his cheek to distract him. Michael looked down at her and she smiled softly. "She will be okay."

The gods know I love Michael, but he can be so aggravating sometimes. Why would anyone say something like that to someone in this kind of situation? I do not need something like that weighing on my soul. Not now. I mean…Did he really think that the thought didn't cross my mind? I just didn't want to think of it. It was way too heartbreaking on top of everything else. The mere possibility curled my stomach into knots and pumped my heart at the speed of light.

I came to a sudden halt, I couldn't move. Frozen stiff I slipped into a trance the air was still and the snow fell thicker. It got so cold that it hurt to breath. I could fell an ancient evil coming near but it wasn't close enough yet to be specific. I came back quickly and spun around to the others watching me and standing still. "Something's coming," I said. Keyoni, Able, Hahn, and Elee closed their eyes as if listening to something. Keyoni shot his eyes open at me. Just as soon as he did so… *Bam!* Something had slammed into me picking me up off the ground and carrying me twenty feet into the black of woods.

I was slammed onto the ground with my arms being pressed into the snow. I looked up to see Antony. "Did you really believe that I would just walk away?" My sword was dropped somewhere along the twenty foot flying lesson then I realized that this vampire curse could be used to my advantage. With my arms being held down it was my best option anyways. I allowed the beast within to come out to play.

My strength escalated and with him still holding a tight grip on my wrists, I pushed back against him. Antony grunted with a surprised yet frustrated look on his face as he began to lose his grip. Then in an instant I head butted him hard enough to make him land flat on his back. In my transformation the cold was unnoticed on my skin. My blood boiled too hot. I huffed rapid as I ripped open my coat and let it drop to the ground keeping my glare on Antony. He stood and wiped away some of the blood that ran down his forehead then looked at it smeared in his hand. I could tell he was confused as to how I got the best of him. Antony scoffed then said, "Well at least now we know that this will be an interesting fight." A satanic smile stretched across his face when the sound of the others fighting their own battle rung through the trees. Obviously, Antony did not come alone. *"I'm okay. You stay and help them."* I thought to myself knowing that Keyoni would hear it.

Antony came at me and I grabbed the chest area of his shirt, spun around then slammed him into a tree. He hissed at me and I growled back. Antony shoved me off of him. With one hand he picked me up by my neck and slammed me to the ground then squeezed with all his might. "If I can't have you…no one can." He grudged through his teeth. The nails on my fingers stretched out like they were spring loaded claws and I swiped his face digging in as much as I could. He screeched then disappeared in the shadows as the sound of more trouble came close. I quickly stood to see myself surrounded by all kinds of creatures. The screeching roars of a dragon filled the sky and with one swoosh over the top of the trees my sword fell from sky and I caught the handle just as a werewolf took the first leap.

Like a flash of lightning I sliced open his chest and the others charged in. Everything I knew about sword fighting came out. Like a samurai keeping up with the speed of light in a lightning storm.

Antony was suddenly behind me. I could feel it. I spun around and my sword clashed against his. He pushed against me crossing our swords then surprised me with a very intense kiss that was all too familiar. The savage that I had awakened to fight wanted him. I couldn't believe it but that part of me still loved him and he was still able to use that in a trance. I began to kiss him back. He lowered his sword as I griped mine. Antony then dropped his sword and entangled both hands in my hair. He slowly pulled away and tilted my head back with one hand as he ran his other hand down my neck. I stared to lower my sword to my side. I couldn't pull myself back. He had truly intoxicated me. Antony's eyes glowed red and his breathing got deeper. His fangs grew and just when he leaned in to make his mark on my neck Able sidelined him with a loud thud and I dropped to my hands and knees.

Antony's body flew like a rag doll and hit a boulder size rock, but he stood up quickly ready to fight back. Lee appeared behind him with a bow and arrow pointed at him and Michael was to Antony's right side glaring intensely while gripping a sword with a harsh squeeze. Hahn came out of the shadows in Hybrid form and stopped two feet from Able's right then Elee came out also Hybrid form on Able's left. Silus and Tyron snuck over to me. Tyron got down on one knee next to me while Silus stood guard in front of us. "You okay?" Tyron asked. I nodded in assurance as I gathered myself then stood up.

Antony grinned at Able. "Hello, Able. I see you have made new and improved friends. Guess that's the plus side about being you. Everyone loves dogs," he said then snickered. Able glowered then gave a snarl and with a gust of wind Keyoni dropped down like a shooting star sending a ripple through the snow on the ground. He landed on one knee with one hand planted firmly on the ground then shot a murderous glare at Antony and stood slowly.

"You need to be smarter about how you pick your fights and who you start them with. Some followers that can actually fight would probably help too," Keyoni said to Antony.

A very creepy dark smile swept across Antony's face and he said, "Don't worry…there's more where they came from. A lot more. Hybrids that no one thought possible." Then he looked over at me and spoke again, "This was just the tip of the iceberg." I eyed him suspiciously and like normal, he disappeared.

"He's good at that," said a voice from behind me and Tyron. Tyron spun around putting me behind him and everyone swiftly drew their attention to the man that came from the shadows. It was Nivoku, Keyoni's brother. Keyoni smiled then walked to him in four, long strides and embraced him with a brotherly hug. Tyron slowly relaxed himself with a look of brief confusion on his face.

They released their hug, then Nivoku said, "It's been too long brother."

"Yeah and you do not age well little brother," Keyoni said with a honry smile. Nivoku socked Keyoni in his shoulder causing him to stumble back.

Keyoni looked at him in surprise then grinned, "You finally got some muscle to pack behind that punch" he said.

Nivoku smiled bright and bold then helped Keyoni up. "Father said there was trouble. He knew you were on your way and didn't want Antony to follow. The only reason it's a safe place is because Antony doesn't know where it is. We moved after he came back for..." Nivoku paused and looked at me hoping that I wasn't taking offense knowing what he was about to say. My eyelids twitched in attempt to glare but that was it. I was really not fazed but he avoided saying her name anyway and continued, "No one knew where we were...until you guys came. It's okay though. Nothing lasts forever. Not even the best-kept secrets. I didn't come alone either. The others are out there keeping watch. We should go now though."

Just as he said that a bald eagle screeched then Nivoku and Keyoni shot panicked looks over to me and...sloosh...a sword was ran through my gut with Antony holding it from behind. I gasped and looked down at the blade. Everyone jumped and Keyoni's eyes became a fiery gold and he thunderously roared. "Nooooo!" Then he began to huff and puff. I pulled the blade forward running the blade through me a couple more inches then hit his face with the back of my head causing him to let go of the sword. As soon as he did I spun around grabbed his jacket with both hands and pulled him into the blade with me.

"Do you really think you can kill me that easily?" I whispered in his ear grudgingly then with one violent kick sent him back into the shadows. I dropped to my side and breathed heavily while my blood began to sew itself into the snow as if I was lying on a red blanket. Keyoni started to rush to me but Nivoku grabbed his arm and Keyoni shot back an infuriated glare at him.

"Not this time brother. You have to let the fury come if you want her to live." Nivoku said

"He's right," Lee agreed. "Her pain will feed the fear which will turn to panic and the panic will become rage then she'll turn into a vampire. This is one time that talking sense into her will do more harm than good," she added.

"Ya, ya! I heard about them," Silus began, "It's the survival instinct of a half-blood vampire. We will have to pull out the sword first. Someone has to hold her arms down and another will have to gag her. The change heals them but pisses them off too. If the change happens while the sword's being taken out and someone gets scratched or bitten…well, what happens is obvious. After she heals she'll pass out then we can get her and us to safety." Everyone gazed in amazement that Silus knew so much and actually sounded smart when he spoke. It didn't seem like smart was his forte. "What! Hey! I read…and listen to other peoples conversations," he said crossing his arms.

Elee got down on her knees behind me. Keyoni knelt down next to Elee and gripped the sword tightly. Michael got down in front of me and Nivoku was at my legs. I looked up at Michael from the corner of my eyes as my breathing intensified. "The change is beginning," Michael told them. Elee untied a leather strip from her arm and curled each end around her hands leaving about six inches free in the middle. Then forced it into my mouth to secure my head down then Elee readied herself and tightly gripped the leather as I bit down. Michael tied my wrists together and held them down into the snow.

Keyoni leaned in then kissed the side of my forehead and whispered *I'm sorry* then jerked the sword from my body, tossed it to Lee's feet, and held down my midsection. I screamed viciously but slightly muffled by the gag. Lee picked up the sword slowly with tears in her eyes. She peered at the sword as she squeezed the handle then it turned into ashes. Tyron and Silus cringed at the sound of my flesh being sliced while Able and Hahn stood on guard. With no control I thrashed about, to break their hold…to tear them apart. The pain is unexplainable to this day, but as the healing took place, the pain slowly began to fade and so did my consciousness.

"We have to move now and fast. Before she starts to wake up, none of them are brave enough to try and get past our barrier," Nivoku said.

Able nodded in agreement then said, "Elee n' Hahn can take Tyron n' Silus on their backs. I'll scout ahead with Nivoku to make sure you're not bein' followed. There's a lot more out there."

"Right, I'll carry her. Lee can take Michael," said Keyoni. Among his many abilities, Keyoni could control how much he transformed. For instance…he could stay in human form and still fly with great speed just not as high. He could even grow his wings anytime at any length so…he sprouted his wings and buffed his beautiful body after lifting me in his arms and bounded up into the night sky.

Keyoni landed lightly in the middle of the village on one knee then stood up slowly as the natives formed a circle around him "You have mastered your powers. I am proud, my son," his father said standing behind him. Keyoni turned quickly. Nivoku's wife, who was also an ancient healer, pushed past the chief and ran to me in Keyoni's arms. She placed her dainty hand just an inch over my stomach then looked up at Keyoni with worry. "Her wound is healed, but the blade was dipped in the poisoned blood of a maenad. She is still fighting for her life and won't be waking up anytime soon. Come with me." Keyoni followed Paelona into a large hut and laid me on a tall bed of stone that was layered with thick fur. Paelona lit some candles by lightly blowing from her hand toward the candles in one swish. The chief and Myrah came in with Lee, Elee, Michael, Hahn, Able, Silus, and Tyron. Paelona pushed her way through them running out to her hut. She frantically searched the hut trying to remember where she hid the painting.

The chief went over to three shelves that were full of clay jars with herbs and oils in them. He picked up a round clay tray then picked some herbs, oil, and a tincture made from St. John's Wart. With a small mortar, he crushed and blended until, turned it into a paste, and then he began to rub the paste around the edges and on top of the wound while chanting in a tune under a slight mumble.

"This will slow down the poison long enough," the chief said. Keyoni looked at him confused.

"Long enough for what?" Keyoni asked.

His father's mind was one of the few he couldn't touch so he couldn't see what was coming. Just then Paelona came in. "I am sorry but it will take weeks before the medicine is ready," she said.

Suddenly Keyoni shot his head over to Able, Myrah, Hahn and Elee. They all closed their eyes and inhaled very deeply. Then they shot their eyes open and looked at each other then back to Keyoni. "Go," he said to them. They all leapt out of the hut and turned into their wolf form and sprinted off.

"There are more coming," Keyoni said.

"More what?" Michael asked.

"More help and," Lee started, "they're being followed. Able, Myrah, Elee, and Hahn are going to meet with two other pack leaders that sent the message to greet our allies then sound the alarm for others to join that have been lurking here for centuries," she said.

"Antony's trying to start a war," Keyoni said then looked at his father, "Beginning with this village. They're after Pan. The protectors are outnumbered and they will get through the barrier." The chief remained calm then walked over to Paelona took her hand, held it gently between both of his then whispered in her ear. A quick jolt rushed through her body then opened her eyes looking at him in aw then the Chief slowly made his way to my side and continued his meditative chant with a smudge stick.

"What just happen?" Silus asked.

"He just made her his successor. It's the only way she can have enough of what you would call majick to get Pan healed sooner. With Paelona's own and what he just gave her, we might actually be able to save Pan sooner than we thought," Keyoni answered.

"I will get started," Paelona said.

Michael step to her then said, "Thank you." She nodded then walked out.

Keyoni turned and looked at his father with sad compassion. Lee turned to Michael, Silus, and Tyron then said, "We should talk to the warriors and figure out our preparation for a strategy." As she walked them out of the hut. Keyoni breathed in slow and deep then exhaled the same while sitting on a large log next to some smaller logs put together for a small fire. He looked at the small logs took another deep breath then spit out a tiny flame that ignited the small logs into a comfortable fire.

"Why?" Keyoni asked as he looked up at his father resting his elbows on his knees and cupping his hands together.

"You are my only son, but I am allowed to choose my successor and we both know it's not what you want. Yes, we disagree on some things. That does not change what I know and I know the pain of losing a woman you love more than yourself. Do not forget that," the Chief said calmly as he laid the smudge stick in a clay bowl and set the bowl inches from the top of my head then sat on a log across from Keyoni. Keyoni hung his head and gazed at the dirt floor.

"When her soul came reborn in the flesh, the true beauty of her soul formed it into the woman I saw when she first got here. The woman I saw looked a lot like your mother when she was young, vibrant and alive," The chief continued. Keyoni looked back up at him with amazement all over his face. "Then I knew why I had to let you go. She has your mother's passion and strong will. The two things I couldn't escape from either," the chief finished then smiled. "Her beauty alone is hard to not be drawn to," he added.

Keyoni smirked. "Thank you," Keyoni said.

His father nodded then said, "Save this village and that will be thank you enough," the chief said. Keyoni gave one nod then stood and they hugged each other then Keyoni left to join the rest.

Keyoni came out of the hut and Tyron was in front of him trying to catch his breath. Keyoni creased his eyebrows in confusion. "We were in the lodge…and…just come on…you are never…gonna believe what just happen." Tyron panted. Keyoni walked ahead with Tyron two steps behind him and into the lodge then stopped frozen and whispered, "A demigod. That's not possible."

Her hair was a mahogany color that curled into long ringlets like fine ribbon her eyes were the color of a sparkling lime. She had fair cream-colored skin and a curvy muscular build. "My name is Ashton. I am the daughter of Athena, among the very few that are left. My mother is the goddess of wisdom in war strategy so trust me, surviving was not the hard part about my life. My mother broke the rules to come to me. I know all the safe routes and places to go. I know how all of them fight and most of their weaknesses. This is not my first battle," she said.

Keyoni looked around at everyone in the room waiting for him to say something then he looked at Ashton and said, "We need all the help we can get." Ashton let out a small smile then exhaled and they all adjourned.

Keyoni's Words

I couldn't escape the gulping fear of losing Pan. Her soul is more fragile than it ever had been. She was all I wanted to think of as I sat among everyone in the lodge. We all discussed many plans and strategies. Spoke of what we knew about our enemies and bickered a little over what would or wouldn't work.

As I sat and listened to Silus emphasize more on the newborns, the feeling of trying to gather one's self when waking only seconds after a very big explosion, almost seemed to be overwhelming me as it inched its way through my body. My eyesight began to blur then came the pressure of two hundred pounds trying to squish my lungs together. I tilted my head back slowly while closing my eyes. Lee looked over at me; sensing what was going on, then she raised her voice among the chattering and stood up quickly and said, "Wait!" Holding a concentrated stare at me, everyone got quiet immediately and fixed their attention on me also.

Lee sat down and crossed her legs. Without needing to close her eyes or say any incantations she stepped inside my head. "What's goin on?" Ashton asked.

"She's trying to get to him telepathically," Michael said. Lee shook her head lightly with a confused troubled look on her face.

"I can't get there, he blocked that part of his mind from me," Lee said.

"Try tapping into just his emotions not his mind," Tyron suggested. Lee closed her eyes and almost seemed to not be breathing. After a few seconds she popped her eyes open and looked at Michael.

"I didn't see it, but I tapped into his emotions and put the pieces together. It was a vision and from the feeling of it…it's all bad," she said.

While they worried and pondered about the Keyoni's out of body absence. I was experiencing it. When I closed my eyes I seemed to be descending through a black hole then in tunnel vision I saw the entrance to where Rahmeeku lived. The door was broke down and there was no light or sound. Just an eerie cold breeze that came from inside.

I stepped through the doorway and walked a couple feet through the long arched passage then stopped to see two of Rahmeeku's magi lying stacked on top of one another with their own spears driven through them to the ground and a large chunk of flesh ripped out of their necks. Not knowing who this vision was coming from began to worry me. The vision quickened my pace and showed me every room in the ransacked place until I got to the altar room. At my feet laid a decapitated vampire. I looked around the destroyed room then saw Rahmeeku standing in front of me. He pounded his staff on the ground then dissipated in a whirlwind suddenly, just as quick, Antony jumped at me savagely and I came out of it.

Lee was still seated in front of me. "What is it?" she asked. I looked at her wide eyed with adrenaline.

"It's Rahmeeku. Antony went after him but I don't know if he's reaching me from this world or the afterlife. As a matter of fact I don't even know who this is coming from. It might not even be him. If I tell you any more than that Antony will see me coming if he's even there," I said.

"We're coming with you," Silus said as he and Tyron stepped forward side by side.

"No. We are living in the, what if, now and if there is a random attack the both of you are gonna be more than needed here," I said to them. I could see the worried look on their faces and hear the millions of excuses running through Lee's head in hopes to raise a good point by arguing, but Tyron gently put his hand on Silus' shoulder and Silus exhaled then stormed out passed me.

Tyron walked to me then said, "Sorry. Rahmeeku is a father to us. Probably more so for him than for me." I nodded then Tyron walked out to find Silus. I looked over at Lee and she nodded. I knew what she wanted to say she knew that I wouldn't listen. I winked with a grin then walked out and took flight with the speed of light.

Rahmeeku's place was just as I had seen in my vision. It was dark, cold and unsettling. The door was broke down like I expected and the two men were in the same way. I didn't even bother with searching any other room and headed straight for the altar room. I stopped about three feet from the door for Antony's scent was strong and seeped through the door thickly.

I huffed and puffed while my eyes blazed with a fiery gold. My fists clinched closed tighter and tighter as my muscles slowly bulged. I squeezed my eyes shut sprung my hands wide open to allow my claws to grow just a little and my breathing quickened. I quickly brought up my arm holding it straight out with the palm of my hand stretching out. My finger bent slightly as if holding a baseball then out came a bursting ball of blue and green fire. It instantly engulfed the door then ignited a few candles still standing a couple of feet behind the door and disappeared. I love being able to do that. It's a rush that no one could understand.

Antony was standing in the middle of the room darkly glowering at me. I stepped into the room cautiously slow. "There's no line you won't cross is there?" I asked rhetorically as I glared back at him, my eyes still blazing.

He snickered then said, "I'm not dumb enough to come to you so…I gave you a good enough reason to come to me. What I don't understand is you knew Rahmeeku wasn't here. You know he's alive yet you still came." Antony's evil stretched across his face in the form of a smile. He knew the fury that resided in me after enduring the pain of Pan's struggle and he was proud. I grinned darkly,

"Once I decide to do something I'm committed to getting it done and I have decided to kill you," I said.

"You let your anger cloud your better judgment," Antony warned.

Meanwhile…Everyone had quickly taken their post. Lee rushed it due to the fact that me being drawn away so abruptly was oddly discomforting and she would find out that she was right to worry.

As soon as I was a decent distance away from the village two werewolves came barreling their way through to Lee and Ashton who had just taken their post outside of the hut that Pan rested in. In a single leap they took human form coming to a skidding halt. They were both young. One of them was pale skinned and had four big scars close to one another down the side of his face like claw markings. The other was big boned and tall with dark caramel colored skin, his chest covered in scars. Both were panting out of breath but the bigger one managed to speak. "They're already here. We have been roaming the west and were supposed to meet some of our allies at the coast, but what we found were our enemies landing ashore and we started our way here. On the way a hawk dropped down a note. The allies are safe and knew of the danger. The bad thing is…they had to land about three thousand miles from where we are now. The enemy was close behind and we have no time," he said.

Lee's eyes got wide like a light bulb had come on. She realized what Antony was doing. Just then a demon dived out of the night sky and grabbed a toddler. Nivoku saw it and immediately leaped into the air taking flight as a Bald eagle big enough to carry a full-grown man. The demon stopped mid air and turned to screech at him.

Nivoku slammed into the demon causing it to drop the child. The child screamed uncontrollably, and then landed on the back of a shape shifter member of the tribe whose form was that of a giant owl. He landed firmly close to the mother and she quickly embraced her son, said thank you, and then fled. The demon hit the ground with Nivoku still on top of him in his eagle form. Nivoku held the wriggling demon down with one talon as it screeched at him. In one quick motion Nivoku dipped his head in and severed the demons' head with one chomp.

Lee could sense them like a hungry bloodhound, making it easier to get past how well they hid in the night sky. She raised her bow and arrow then released the arrow. It silently disappeared in the sky like a butterfly amped with the speed of light. A screeching cry of agony called out and a demon dropped to the ground. Lee pulled out three more arrows and used them all at once dropping three more demons.

Ashton reached behind her and pulled out what looked like to Lee was a wide steel handle about two feet long with garnets making the design of a rose with a round onyx in the middle of it and a four edged four inches long spear head. "What are you gonna do with that? Kill a cat?" Lee said dryly sarcastic. Ashton smiled then pushed on the onyx with her thumb and the blade of a sword shot out. A demon swooped down at her and in one glide the demon split in half horizontally. In hearing the fearful screams of a woman Ashton looked ahead. Another demon was chasing down a woman thirty feet away from her. Ashton double clicked on the onyx and the spearhead shot out connected to a coiled chain. It pierced through the demon's back and opened up inside of him then she yanked violently pushing the onyx twice again. The spearhead coiled itself back into the handle leaving the demon lying motionless with a hole in his back eight inches wide and four inches deep of mangled flesh.

Lee looked in aw then said, "I like you." Ashton smiled proudly then grabbed a dagger from her hip and threw it in Lee's direction. The dagger flew within an inch of missing her throat then Lee heard the sound of something choking down water. She turned quickly to see a foot soldier demon lying on the ground with the dagger in his neck. Lee looked back at Ashton smiling again. "Thanks," Lee said. Ashton nodded. "I have to guard Pan. You go find Paelona and keep her safe. We need her to save Pan. I'm gonna try and contact Keyoni." Ashton Nodded then ran off through the scattered crowed.

Back at Rahmeeku's...I glared Antony's comment in suspicion. Then as loud as a banshee Lee's voice came through. My eyes rolled back and my eyelids fluttered. "It's an ambush! Get out of there now!" she called out sending images of the fight. I shot my eyes open. The flames blew out and Antony was gone. I could still smell him though and knew he lurked in the shadows.

"I take it that you figured out my plot," Antony said. His voice echoed from the dark.

"It was all a distraction. I should've known that you were incapable of being honest," I said eyeing the shadows in case he decided to leap.

"Everything I told her was true aside from one thing...This was never about her killing Adrianna. I love my daughter. I am at least capable of that. No...This is about me using Adrianna to kill her," Antony said.

My eyes got wide with concern and anger "Now you're trying to start fight on sacred ground. Don't push me or we'll both be in trouble," I warned then swished my left hand up at the candle chandelier igniting the candles. The room lit up bright and five darts came at me sticking into my lower back. "Aaaahhh!" I cried out and dropped down to my knees as I reach behind me to pull the darts out then Antony leapt at me from a corner behind me.

Just as sudden, a booming wave shook the room knocking Antony into a table. I covered my face to shield from the debris. Rahmeeku's voice thundered, "Anthony!" Rahmeeku was standing at the door and Antony stood himself up fumbling about a little bit. "How dare you spill blood in my house? Have you forgotten the meaning of sacred! First you kill two men them impersonate me in his mind to spill more blood in my house!" Rahmeeku shouted then disappeared and reappeared just as quickly right in front of Antony. "I don't deal in death but you will feel my wrath," he said in a lower tone then gripped Antony's neck and squeezed. Rahmeeku's eyes speared rage at him as he gasped for air in apparent pain and Antony began to slowly flicker like a flame in the wind then disappeared.

Rahmeeku took a deep breath and exhaled then came to my side and helped me up then walked me to a nearby couch. "I sent him to another realm but I can't hold him there for too long before he finds his way out," Rahmeeku said as he fumbled about his tinctures and herbs in a hurry.

Back at the village, Silus speared a soldier demon through the eye then felt a hand on his shoulder. He pulled out a knife then spun around ready to lodge it into whatever touched him. "Whoa! It's me!" said Michael breathing heavily. Silus relaxed his arm down and put the knife away.

"They're just and soldier demons. This battle is a decoy. I have to go to Lee and help her guard Pan. You and Tyron go find Ashton and Paelona," Michael told Silus.

The wind began to pick up and they could hear screeching above them. They looked at each other then slit in opposite directions. Silus ran passed Tyron as he was splicing a machete through a fury. "Tyron!" Silus called. "We gotta find Ashton!" Tyron caught up with Silus immediately and they headed toward Paelona's hut.

Little did Michael know what really ran in his blood after saving Lee from the Vampire attack. Michael arrived to see that Lee was distracted by a pack of soldier demons, enough for a young girl to slip past. Michael saw the young girl slip into the hut Pan rested in then, swift and quiet, Michael slipped in after her only to see her lift a dagger at Pan's chest. Michael's anxiety became immediate blind rage and he leapt at the girl slamming her to the ground. Michael then struggled to hold her down but…then he saw her face. She looked remarkably, a lot like Pan and he knew who she was. This realization made him pause and his pausing made her pause, "Adrianna," he whispered then a riveting unseen force pushed Michael off of her and she tried to go for Pan again. Michael caught himself skidding back a couple feet then charged at her side in a single bound. He slammed into her and when they both hit the ground she got up on her hands and knees and crawled toward the dagger. Michael got up on his hands and grabbed her ankle right as she grabbed the dagger and in the blink of an eye, Adrianna lodged the dagger into Michael's chest. Lee teleported into the hut and saw Adrianna fade away while Michael lay on the floor curled up fighting for his life.

Lee was by him in an instant. Panic was trying to over amp her heart but she did her best to stay calm though it was evident that Michael was dying. She helped him slowly roll over. "Michael? Michael, look at me." Michael's eyelids fluttered then lifted hesitantly and his vision cleared. Lee was leaning the top half of her body on his chest with her arms holding her up, giving only a couple inches between their faces. Michael grinned slightly then raised his hand to rest on her face while his thumb caressed her cheek and Lee caressed his hand with hers. It was apparent that Lee was fighting the persistence of painful tears.

"I did what I was here to do. Pan will live. I…will always love… you." After Michael said that, his arm went limp and his thumb stopped caressing. Lee rested Michael's hand on his chest and the other as well then gently kissed him one last time then sat back and gulped down the stabbing pain.

"Lee! Michael! They're leaving," Tyron called from outside the hut. Tyron burst into the hut with Silus, Ashton, and Paelona behind him. "They all just took off. They're…" Tyron began then saw Michael, "gone." Lee kept her back to them so as not to show them the tears she lost control of.

Paelona walked up behind her and knelt down then put a hand on each side of her upper arms. "Come. You must gather yourself," Paelona said softly then gently helped her to her feet, "Lee needs to be in peace. You all stay and prepare Pan for travel. Don't leave Michael there," she said as she walked Lee out.

As I lay only clinched my teeth at the stinging pain of the darts being plucked out of me, Lee's thought's came in like a herd of elephants on a stampede as Rahmeeku pulled out the last one.

"Aaaahhhh!" I yelled, arching my back and jolting my head back. Then as he applied medicine to relieve the pain, I plopped my head back down on my arm and said, "Something's wrong. Lee can't control her mind."

"Yes. Something had gone wrong, but it is something that cannot be fixed…yet," Rahmeeku said.

I began to try and push myself back up saying, "Pan? Is she—"

"Alive?" Rahmeeku interrupted.

"Yes, her life was spared because Michael gave his." My eyes shot wide open when he said this and watered with fierce anger and sorrow. "Adrianna is more dangerous and cunning than you all realize," Rahmeeku added.

I creased my eyebrows inward and my eyes went to a vengeful glare. "But she's not invincible," I said a deeper tone. "You must think wise on this Keyoni. Pan is still in grave danger if she stays there and these darts have been dipped in an elixir that will temporarily handicap your ability to fully transform. Hunting down Adrianna, Antony or both will not only get you killed but break the balance and defeat our purpose. Lee needs your inner strength more than ever right now. Don't let your anger cloud your reasoning." I hated it with a passion but...Rahmeeku was right. Though evil beckoned to my rage, I calmed myself.

Rahmeeku finished patching me up then said, "You'll have to teleport to get back to the village. Your allies will be there in two days. From there all of you will head west for three more days and on the fourth day head south until you are deeply surround by willows and swamp area. There you will be meeting with some...beings that can help you more than I can and you must be careful. Not all of them will want anyone but you there, you must not separate. One unparticular knows your coming do not bother looking for him because he will find you. He's good at that." I nodded in assurance that I understood his instruction then slowly stood up and put on a dark blue button up loose shirt that Rahmeeku gave to me then he tossed me a black trench coat a little loose also but hey...at least I could breath.

"Now go. Your time is short." I slowly rested my head back as my eyes rolled and my arms slowly raised to shoulder height then a whirling blaze of blue and green fire engulfed me then looking as if I was being sucked into a pea size black hole, me and the inferno were gone.

I knew who we'd be meeting up with, and I can't say that I like it too much. He's unpredictable and has never taken sides since he escaped the devil's grasp. Yes...I'm talking about the Demon among the first seven. It's hard to call it, him. Especially since I considered him to be nothing more or less than pure evil. No gender; just a mass of evil with the exception of his slight capability to feel anything beyond hate.

Like a star falling from the sky, I returned to the village with an earth-quivering landing. I stood to see the people surrounding me then turned to see the others come out of the hut. Lee stood in front of them. I walked over to her then said, "I'm so sorry."

Then my eyes began to water. She plopped her forehead on my chest and I held her for a few seconds then she let go and took a step back wiping her tears away, "We can't leave him here," she said.

I nodded then turned to the people. "There is a place south of here where some of our allies have been hiding for the past few centuries. Take only what you need. We leave at the brake of dawn." I said with a slightly raised voice to make sure they all heard me, and then we all began to prepare for travel.

I helped move Michael into another hut where Lee cast a spell to make his rest ageless then we wrapped him up and I went back to be with Pan. As I sat by her side caressing her hand the fear had grown more and more. My breathing quickened and I my blood ran hot, but I got the feeling that there was someone nearby. They came closer and I knew who it was.

"Come in, but be careful with your words. I know what you've been hiding," I said and Ashton stepped in.

"I'm sorry," she said. I stood up and walked toward her stopping only inches away from her.

"You have your mother's trickery and lust…daughter of Aphrodite," I said taking one step closer. I dipped my head down to her left ear as I carefully placed my right hand on her waist then said lightly, "But it is lust I can use." She inhaled jaggedly and slowly closed her eyes.

I then spun her to press my front into her back then whispered in her other ear. "Did you really put that much hope into me not knowing?"

She began to breath harder and harder loosing the ability to try and unwrap my arms around her leaving me free to glide one hand up to her breast. "Yes," she faintly let out.

I kissed her neck lightly twice then asked, "You know what you have to do now, don't you?" she nodded twice and as I glided my hand up to her neck I whispered one more time, "You know…you're not the only one with a lustful gift?" Then I spun her around again and slammed her back against a wall with one hand tightly gripping her neck. "Give me one good reason why I shouldn't tear you apart and turn you into ashes!" I grudgingly said. I blackened my eyes then growled low.

Startled, Ashton choked out. "Because I can still help." Knowing she was right I let go and stepped back calming myself. Ashton caught her breath than said, "I also have a message from Lee. Able communicated telepathically and said that him, Myrah, and a few others would meet us half way." I nodded in response then sat next to Pan with my back to her. "With a reputation like mine I didn't think that you guys would let me tag along and I didn't tell you guys about her and the demon because I didn't know he was still around. There's no more reason than that. Please allow that even someone like me can change. I am still learning," she said.

I stood up and turned to her quickly, "That does not excuse what you did! You brought Adrianna right to her knowing what she was gonna do and you actually believed you could stop her!" I said sternly with fury in my eyes. She came close and grazed her hand on my cheek.

"I told you…I know what I have to do. Though, I wish you would let me do more," she said dropping her hand to the side and grinning. "I owe Pan my life anyways so if I die my debt is repaid," she said then walked out.

The next day, we all made our way as soon as the sun stretched its first light across the sky. Able and the rest joined up with us when they said they would with food, water, horses and two carriages to carry Michael and Pan. After we ate…Able, Myrah, Hahn and Elee introduced the soldiers and warriors. They were from all over. A lot of them were from the underground hide out we were staying at but what really surprised me was that there were even humans ready and willing to do the impossible. I went over everything with them then we reorganized everything and traveled on south.

About two months had gone by and spring was coming through. We were lucky enough to avoid the rain but the dark clouds that follow threaten our luck. One day while we all sat to eat a quick snack, Silus and Tyron inconspicuously sat near me. "You know as well as we do that we're getting closer to our destination," Tyron said.

I nodded once. "That shape shifter has been following us since yesterday," I told them then looked back at Ashton who had been eyeing us. She knew as well as the rest of us then she smiled and winked.

There was no actual plan and I don't know what she was thinking of doing. Back at the hut we both knew what she had to do but how was the mystery. She knew how block those kind of thoughts from me. As a matter of fact she knew how to hide any thought she wanted to hide except for her guilty conscious. After what she did I didn't like her hiding anything from me. The last thing she tried to hide got someone killed. I can honestly say that I don't trust her. I can handle whatever comes but…would rather not take the risk. In this case the risk is necessary. I kept my thoughts safe from Lee. She might be an angel, but she's got a temper from hell and it was still screaming for revenge. I knew that I couldn't tell her about Ashton. Lee would've killed her and as wrong as this may sound…the only reason I cared was because she was the only way we could make friends with a Demon.

He wouldn't even exist if not for Pan. In the beginning of all this, Pan knew that there had to be a balance for everything. Good and Evil, Love and Hate, Male and Female. The list goes on. Sometimes the worst is as much a necessity as is the best. I knew we needed her because Pan's the only other being that could speak his language. Obviously Pan can't do any talking for a while and me…well let's just say that the demon and I have mutually agreed to hate each other, leaving…again…Ashton as our only hope. If she stays true to her word, everything should go well.

"What was that about?" Tyron asked.

"You and she aren't…" Silus started to ask when Tyron read my mind and slapped the back of his head.

"Don't worry about it. Let everyone know that we need to get moving. We are going further south until the sun begins to set. Then we'll stop to rest for the night," I told them then walked away toward

Lee. She kept post by Michael's carriage. "How are you holding up?" I asked.

"I have been trying to find were his soul could be resting but still nothing. I don't understand," Lee said, "I'm sorry. When we get to safer grounds I'll try to get a hold of John. We're getting ready to move out. At night fall we'll rest. I just wanted to make sure that you were okay." She smiled at me assuringly and I kissed her forehead. While we walked on Pan's powers were growing more powerful than any of us knew it could. Her strong will was pushing it harder than ever and she began to heal.

That night…the thick clouds that had been chasing us finally caught up. The rain began pour thickly. We set up camp just in time though and while the others slept I took watch over them. The rain felt like warm teardrops and the cold air that everyone took shelter from was like fresh summer air to me. Thunder rolled and I looked up thinking to myself that this storm wasn't just a storm. Nature herself knew what was going on and she was not happy about it. Mankind to this day had continued to abuse her worse and worse. They have the power of control over their own freedom yet; good wealth and lust consume them. It pains me to see it. In my premonitions I had seen all the pain and suffering that is so common in these modern times. The only thing that hasn't changed for better or worse is the greedy selfishness of those who consider themselves upper class.

Oh I would give anything to have Pan at my side right now. I thought to myself. You would think that after so many years of being without her before would've made it easier.

The rain paused and as I looked toward the cloud-shadowed sky, I felt the cold air lightly shift and I knew who was creeping away in the shadows. "Ashton," I said. She stopped and turned to me. "I have to go alone. Things will be a lot less complicated for you guys if I talk to him first. Find out where his allegiance lies. Being the daughter of a goddess who is known for her perfect seduction really helps. I can persuade anyone and anything. It's where my reputation came from. I can honestly say that you give me a decent amount of competition on that though," Ashton said letting out a small grin. I smiled back with a very light chuckle then nodded and she disappeared into the night.

I waited in the shadows until I knew she wasn't near then Able quietly crept out of the dark as Nivoku in eagle form swooped down and perched on my shoulder. Able took his human form. "You really don't trust her do you?" Able asked.

I lightly shook my head. "She doesn't know that I told you guys about her. So don't make a sound. Able you stay on guard and let no one see you. Nivoku I need you to shape shift into something that is small enough to catch the slightest whisper and no attention."

"Okay," said Able and then he transformed. Nivoku soared away taking form of the great white owl. I watched him soar away wondering to myself of the centuries to come. The things I've seen. Then…a thick drop of rain splashed on my cheek reminding me of here and now reality. I had no time to dwell on the future any more than I had time to think about the past. As the rain showered me I couldn't feel the chill of the cold soaking. Faint steam rolled off of me but became thicker as I worried more about the reality I was dealing with and I had to see her.

I appeared suddenly in front of Silus and Tyron guarding Pans carriage. They jumped ready to attack until they realized it was me. "You can't be doin that man. I think my heart jumped out of my chest. Careful where you step it's down there somewhere," Silus stressed. Tyron and I snickered at him.

"You need somethin?" asked Tyron.

"I just need some time alone." I gestured toward Pan.

"Ah. Got it," Tyron said then he and Silus walked away. I stepped in and sat next to her amazed. She was out of deaths grasp it seemed and still trying to figure out a way to get past the poison that kept her so out of reach. I realized that she had more power than anyone knew possible. We all under estimated the true powers angels and demons posses. When her mother and father made her they combined more than imaginable. I lay next to her wondering if she would come back the same or was this more potent power made of pure evil. As I thought the possibilities I eventually fell asleep but it was interrupted. I heard Paelona's voice outside the carriage arguing with Silus and Tyron. I poked my head out. "What's going on?" I asked.

Paelona held up a vile, "The medicine is ready," she said. I sat aside holding the curtain open. She came in and sat on the other side of Pan.

"Hold her head up," she demanded. I did, so then she carefully opened Pan's mouth and poured the medicine in. I stretched her neck out to get the medicine to flow down her throat.

"Now what?" I asked as I lay Pan's head down.

"That part was left out. Now, we wait," she answered. I did not like this answer but it was all I had. So I anxiously waited not sleeping for even a second.

The next day Lee of course twenty questioned me and she had her doubts but settled with my answers. I told her everything except for Ashton's deception. In two-days time they came back as we were continuing our long journey. Nivoku in his usual eagle form swooped down into the trees and came out a man walking along side of Able also now a man. I had everyone stop and rest while I talked with Nivoku and Able. "There are all kinds of creatures there. It's almost like a refugee camp. None of them seem to have any alliances on the outside. They like to keep to themselves. If there are any real bad ones, than they've already been recruited. His stench was still lingering in the air." Able said. My eyebrows curved inward from concern and my hate for him.

"Antony knows where we will be, and he's planning another attack."

"How do you know he'll attack there?" Able asked.

"Because I know him." I answered then said, "We'll have to worry about that later right now I need to know what's goin on with Ashton."

"Well she did it and it seems she is still faithful to the cause. The demon's in love and the two of them left yesterday morning with two hundred others. Shape shifters, vampires, werewolves, demons, faeries and elves," Nivoku informed.

I looked at him in surprise and asked, "Elves? I thought they disappeared years ago. Before Pan was even born. How did they hide out for this long?"

"I don't know that, but I do know what I saw and if I was you… the only one I would be worried about is the demon. Remember it was demons that charged the attack on the village. We have to be careful. They'll be here by night fall," said Able. I nodded then looked over at Pans carriage. She would be the only one that could predict his every thought out moment. I was being tested. I took a deep breath, and we began preparation. I gave Lee the details then took flight to watch for them from the sky. I needed to think.

A New Alliance

They arrived when Nivoku said they would. Before they reached the camp, I met with them at the edge of the forest. The demon had taken human form but I still knew it was him. I came down in front of him like a shooting star. He didn't stir. When the fire cleared he grinned darkly at my glare. "Come on Key. You know I could care less about Antony's war. Being a part of his vengeance does not benefit me. Those demons were not acting on any order of mine," he said

"What name are going by now?" I asked not being able to argue his statement.

He smiled pleased with himself then said, "Nomed."

I snickered then said sarcastically, "Oh, how ironic." Nomed stepped close to me and stared me down.

"I know that you have no reason to trust my alliance with you but...you can trust that I am a very selfish being and taking sides in good seems to favor my existence more so than the other side. You know that I will always care more for my own than any. That, you can trust." Knowing he was right gave me an odd kind of hope. As much as he loved only himself he help us with anything to save his own life and name for that matter.

"You do realize that none of this will make any difference. The Vatican has prevailed and will cover up everything in detail. In five hundred or less this will all become children's bedtime stories, myth and fantasy."

I glared back at him deeply. "Your point?" I said.

His face went blank giving me a sign that his next question was truly innocent curiosity. "Why do it at all?" he asked.

"So that when the time is *right* we will still be around to set truth straight and make the wrong, right." I gulped before saying, "Your existence is and...will be proof that *some* evil is necessary." I hated to say it but I had to give his selfishness what he was looking for...inspiration for himself. Yes I will not lie...we were desperate. His evil grin turned into a self-gratified smile. My eyes went black.

"Relax." Nomed smirked. "Your people will be safe," he said with a serious tone. A man appeared in a serene glow that engulfed him to blend in to the background. The glow lightly faded to show his form. He was like a moving painting. "This is Deardrin. He is the elven elder. The elven have arranged a safe haven for your people," Nomed said. A demons word is hard to take, but Deardrin would have argued if Nomed was lying. The elven have always been known for their honesty.

"We will be leaving at dawn," Deardrin said. I nodded then turned to walk away when he said..."You have not the slightest idea of what she really is. Pandora is more than you could ever perceive and nothing of what you think you know." I stopped dead in my tracks like being frozen in time. "You know how precious she is but you have no idea how dangerous she will become if you do not wake her. She is healed but her soul is hostage. That side of death is fragile. Pandora is in a place where she can be distracted even changed...she is more vulnerable than ever," Deardrin finished then I turned to him.

"And how am I supposed to do that?" I asked with a hint of frustration in my tone. "By trusting the most unreliable." I knew what he meant. I glanced over at Nomed than looked down to the ground with a deep sigh.

"He is the only one that can freely step onto both grounds," Deardrin emphasized. I yet again couldn't argue and that alone was frustrating but I swallowed my pride turned and nodded from my shoulder. The understanding was a silent agreement but an agreement nonetheless.

I said nothing to no one, keeping my mind shut off from any outside effects. I had to calm the anxiety of trusting a demon, with Pans soul in a place I can't get to. He will have free reign.

Nomed did what he was good at. He slipped past everyone undetected. It was the only way to go. Lee would have killed him without thinking twice. I slowly walked to where Pan rested Silus tried talking to and his brother questioned my non-responsive concerned gaze. But they knew that my night visits with Pan was normal and tonight…to them I was just stressed by recent and future events.

What really troubled me was the unpredictable nature of Nomed. As great as my ability to see the far and near future was, some minds like Ashton and Nomed were not in sight. Their unpredictability made it impossible. I could see things that were certain and un-changing. Not knowing the outcome bothered me deeply. Would Pan have agreed if it was me lying there? Would she be so willing to? Then it hit me. If she didn't trust Nomed to some extent, she would not have granted him the evil immortality he was given. She knew who he was then. Something made her choose him and that I had to trust. That's what love is. Trust in your partner's decision no matter how much doubt you have and the willingness to understandingly forgive if they are wrong. No matter how much you don't like it.

I pulled back the curtain of the wagon still standing outside of it. Nomed, of course was already there. Patiently awaiting my signal, but I knew better. Lee had never been okay with me being troubled so as I expected she was close behind. Nomed disappeared when he heard her soft voice. "You have cut me off from your mental state and I understand that, because you need to be left alone from time to time but…

the eyes are windows to the soul. You say that there is more to it than I would like to know," she said.

"I will be fine. I just need to be left alone," I said. Lee had seen many times when I needed that space to be free and therefore she knew that this was one of those times. Luckily she questioned no more and hesitantly walked away. Normally she's quick to offer condolence but she listened. I knew she was smart enough to know that I was hiding something but she trusted it to be for a good reason.

I stepped into the wagon and took a deep breath as I glared darkly into Nomed's eyes while he reappeared. Making a point to remind him that anything other than what was expected would end him permanently. He held up both hands briefly and said, "Her soul is stronger where she is. If you think I can play games with her and get away with it, you only doubting her." He was right. I scowled than took a deep breath and sat down on the built in bench. I gave the okay and Nomed straddled himself on top of her. He gently scooped his hand behind her head and lifted it about an inch then used his other hand to carefully pry open her mouth. In doing so, he brought his mouth only a fraction of an inch away from her mouth, and they both began to glow with a purplish light surrounding them. Suddenly in an instant he was sucked into her and disappeared from my sight.

Now, back to my own words...

Purgatory is not so bad when you're allowed some much needed free time to heal, concentrate, and rebuild strength in ways never thought possible.

My powers were growing to a new level. In a place consumed by darkness I was able to surround myself with the brightest light. I wanted to get back where I was needed, but the swords curse had screwed that up. I knew of Ashton's deception, but anger and vengeance was far from my comprehension at this time. I just wanted to get back to where I belonged...at Keyoni's side.

Before I knew it the light had started to dim. "If you think your being sneaky you are sadly mistaken," I said with my eyes still closed.

"You know...one of these days I will find a way around you," Nomed said.

"That I have no doubt in," I responded.

"Mmm." He smirked.

"I was beginning to wonder when Keyoni would let you in. I knew he was stubborn but I didn't think that he would have to be convinced by another," I said.

Nomed smiled "Don't take it personally. He just despises every fiber of my evil existence," he said in a sarcastic tone. I giggled lightly at how Nomed enjoyed it so much.

"So are you gonna get me out of here or not?" I asked. Nomed smiled then jerked my body against his.

"Hold tight. It's a bumpy ride," he said. Then before I knew it I was gasping for air as my eyes shot open. Keyoni at my side, I sure, but I think I heard him gasp lightly with me. Nomed slowly took form out of what seemed to be a deep purple mist.

Keyoni was so overjoyed that his eyes were heavy with tears. I smiled lightly. In quickness he scooped me up in his arms and held tighter than ever before. He exhaled then said in a whisper, "I thought I had lost you forever."

"Keyoni. I can't breathe," I said. He loosened his grip and lightly smiled as I faced him. I caressed the left side of his face with my hand then I put my forehead on his. "Even in death I will never be lost," I said.

Sensing the life back in me, Lee flung the curtains to the wagon open and barged her way to way to me. She slammed into me almost knocking me down and embraced me with a warm hug. Lee pulled away from me. "I'm sorry but I couldn't contain myself so I ran and everyone noticed. There might a crowd out there," she said. I grinned then with Keyoni's help got out of the wagon to see my friends in front and center of an entire tribe. Silus smiled brightly and Tyron swept me off my feet as he hugged me and spun around once.

Myrah hugged me gently and said, "It's good to see ya, love." Then she let go lightly and kissed my forehead so soft. Able grabbed me and engulfed me in his arms then squeezed the breath right out of me.

"What took you so long?" he asked sarcastically after letting go.

I smirked then took a breath. The air was moist but sweet. The willow trees glowed in the shimmering lights of fireflies and the muggy water took on a new beauty sparkling as the fireflies danced over the surface. The clouds covered the night sky blanketing the stars from sight and the moons beam relentlessly struggled through the thickness.

"The elven have scattered themselves around the world to take, those who would follow, to safety," Keyoni informed me.

"Okay. We need to gather everyone else and bring them to the clearing nearby," I ordered.

"But Pan, we don't have much more time. We need to head to the pier and set a course for Asia," Lee said. They all looked at me in question. "Look. Traveling by ship will take too long and is far too dangerous. They'll make fish food out of us on the open waters. While in purgatory John paid me a visit..."

"And?" Tyron egged on.

"Let's just say that I learned something new," I finished.

I stood on top of a small mound dirt and grass. "I need all of you to gather around me. Get as close to one another as possible," I called out. They closed in forming a circle. I closed my eyes and steadied my breathing then tilted my head. My hands came out from my side about four inches. I began speaking an incantation in Latin. "Spiritus est. Demones sunt in tenebris non maneat. Aperiam in via tuta est duplex." For you I'll translate..."Spirit of light. Demons of the dark. Pave the safe path to our destination." I repeated it as the wind picked up. My hair whipped around my face and my eyes rolled back. I opened my eyes glowing white and faced forward slowly raising my arms above my head. The wind gust picked up forming a cyclone around us all. Keyoni shot his head in my direction with awe and slight concern in his eyes.

"Paaan. What are..." he tried call out as I brought my hands together in a violent clap. Speaking the words even louder, the cyclone turned into a black mist, closed in and absorbed us all. It shrunk down to pea size then sent a shock wave fifteen miles in every direction before dissipating.

To everyone's surprise, we landed in the desert just two miles in front of Cairo, Egypt. The sand stopped mid air and fell back down to where it came from. I slowly lowered my arms and brought the color back to my eyes while coming out of my trance. Everyone cautiously stood straight looking around them then they began to analyze themselves. Everyone was dressed in appropriate attire so as not to stand out too much.

They all looked at me, but Keyoni beat them to it. "What was that?" he said in a sarcastic curious tone.

I grinned then said, "It's pretty much a direct line to John."

"Well, next time...How bout given us some fair warning, love," Able said as he walked toward my left.

"Sorry," I said smirking. "Everyone listen up!" I spoke loud so others who were further away from me could hear, "Cairo is just two miles that direction. Keyoni, Nomed, Hahn, Myrah, and I will gather supplies, food, and definitely water from there. The rest of you stay here until we return. The people would not take kindly to an army walking into their city. When we get back we'll head out to find a good place to set up camp. There we will figure out how to get to Southwest Asia." I instructed. Keyoni looked at me smiling; impressed by the way I took charge. "You look good," he said. I just smiled at him then looked down as I slid my hand in his. Underneath his silky skin, even in the desert heat, his heat was bearable. The energy that flowed through him was still so potently amazing. We clasped our hands together then started walking.

"So what happened to you?" Hahn asked.

"Anubis," I answered. They all stopped including Keyoni. Their faces were full of surprise and confusion all at once. He was among the very few that they didn't believe in. There has been any evidence or sightings for that matter even in the supernatural realm. "His job is to not be seen. It's the element of surprise. You will never see him until he's right in front of you. Even then, you have to believe in him to see him."

"Did you talk to him?" Lee asked.

"Well John found me, not that it was hard for him to do that is his specialty. He told me that Anubis wanted to discuss something. So I did as John instructed and blindly believed. Anubis appeared right in front of me. It was startling. He is huge and the jackal head is a little scary. He said that the decision of my soul's fate was hard but not impossible. John was worried that someone would get hold of my soul so he took me to the only one that could protect me. Then Anubis emphasized that sending me anywhere would have been all bad and in limbo you would never have found me. Since he couldn't put me back in my body he put me somewhere that would be easy enough for the right person to find me. I don't even know where I was," I told them.

We all started walking again. "And he knew it would be him? Why not John or me?" Keyoni asked with a little frustration in his tone while pointing to Nomed.

"I don't think he knew who it would be, but he knows that you can't step beyond purgatory's deepest dark. Only a demented soul can find a place like that."

"Oh, so I'm not demented enough. I'm gonna have to work on that," Keyoni said sarcastically

"You're demented enough for me, babe," I remarked then smiled. Keyoni grinned.

When we got to Cairo the town was buzzing with people living their lives and making their money to survive. Like in any place it had its fair share of beggars. We gave them what we had and made our way to the food stands. There we decided to split up and meet back at the fruit stand we stood in front of. I bought a camel with and packed it with fruit and veggies then began to make my way back to the fruit stand when I heard a women say…"You see everything yet know nothing." I stopped and looked to my side where the women stood at the entrance of a walk way. Her mouth and hair was covered with a black shimmering cloth that draped around the rest of her body.

"Excuse me?" I asked politely.

"You have no reason to trust therefore I am not asking…step inside my home." She gestured down the walk way. I was hesitant but curiosity took over. Who was she and how did she know anything about me. I tried to read her but she hides her inner self well. We got to a small arched door and chiseled on the frame were the same exact symbols as the Egyptian pillow that was beneath my head when I woke up at the underground hide out. I tied the camel to a half-inch-thick ring connected to a four inches thick at three feet tall pole in the ground. "Someone came a long way for it. To ensure that while you rest no would step inside your head," she said as I stepped in the house. I knew she was talking about the pillow and apparently reading my thoughts. No one has ever done that without me knowing. Her powers were ancient even beyond me. So curiosity kept me there.

I looked around and saw alchemist tools and old books stacked under falling piles of dusty scrolls. The place was disorganized and papers with writing of all kinds of languages some older than my soul were scattered all over. Herb bottles were on shelves some on their side but...one bottle particularly...caught my attention. It was empty but still glowed bright and it was the same shape as the elixir that I drank. "I am neutral. I have never taken any side of good or evil. The threat is more immanent. I will do my part although I had hoped that I would be younger when this time came," she said. Then she removed her shawl from her head revealing her ringlet curly hair that even in a braid was just barely touching the floor as well as the rest of her face. She did not seem as old as she said she was her face was that of a thirty-five-year-old. Her complexion was a light brown and her eyes were a dark brown outlined with black.

"You misunderstand the reasons you are so important. You have forgotten," she said.

I stepped closer to her then asked. "Who are you?"

She slightly grinned then sat down, at the only clean table in the place, while gesturing me to sit in the chair across from her. I sat down "Nephora. I am the one everyone comes to for an absolution, questions unanswered, or to heal fatal wounds. When Michael came to me hoping that you would remember who you are but I warned him that some things can only be brought back by you," she informed me.

I looked at Nephora as if waiting for her too tell me what she wasn't saying but it was quiet. I threw up my hands then said, "I have had more lies and truth than I know what to do with! How is that you know me so well and yet I know nothing about you! How come I can't read you and what the hell am I supposed to remember!" My tone colored with more confused frustration.

"I am older than your soul. I was there when your soul made its first transition onto this planet. I know who and where everyone is at all times and to your last question...there would be nothing I could say to force your memory to work. You know what you have to do. You knew when after you drank the elixir, but your human fear compels you not to search much further. You wanted to forget so you did; now if you want to remember you have to want the memory. Here's some advice...start by admitting to yourself that your fear of painful emotion is holding you back then we can go from there," Nephora answered calmly.

I was confused again, "We?" I asked.

"If you want to do this right and in reasonable time then you will need my help," she said then the door slowly opened.

Keyoni stepped in, took one look at her then stretched his arms wide open. "Nene!" he called with a bright smile. She softly smiled back then hugged him. He squeezed her tight picking her up off of her feet.

Keyoni set Nephora down then she put her hands on his shoulders and said, "Oh it's good to see you, child. Although you have grown well. Maybe you aren't such a child anymore."

"Yeah, when he's sleeping," Lee said standing behind Keyoni. The hugged each other like a mother holding her daughter.

"I really do hate to interrupt the happy family reunion but we are quickly running out of time." I said, still frustrated then walked out and untied my camel while Nephora packed her belongings. Keyoni trotted to me staying two steps behind.

"You okay?" he asked trying to hold back a honry grin and I swear I could see it from the back of my head so I did my best to not scream at him. "I hate being confused!" I said with aggravation very vivid in my tone and kept walking. Keyoni's grin turned into a smile as he kept pace behind me.

I couldn't figure it out. If I am suppose to be some great and powerful being destined to save the earth than why do I have such a crappy memory? Keyoni walked to my side and looked at him with a lingering question in my eyes. "What is it?" he asked.

"She knew the ones who birthed my soul. How come I was never told about her?" I replied.

"You really don't know do you?" he said seemingly not surprised.

I shook my head just so slight. "Okay, look. I want to tell you everything but this kind of past and the situations that involve certain people is perceived differently by each person. You need to have your own feelings on the way you see it. Not on what I or anyone else sees and feels. You're not being lied to just not told everything. We weren't sure because none of us were there. We have just heard rumors and stories along with seeing incoherent thoughts from time to time. So you won't get the whole truth you're looking for anyways." His logic was overwhelming. I had no choice but to force a great deal of patience on myself.

I wanted to argue, but I knew it wouldn't help anything like I wanted it too. I figured I would try to calm my struggle with curiosity by changing the subject.

"So...How did you lose me to Antony?" I asked.

He hung his head a little then said, "I'm not surprised you don't remember that. We were in the middle of a war. You were reborn on earth to keep you safe but you had full memory and a shitty family. When you were fifteen, I...died." I my head halfway to the side looking at him in surprise and he continued. "You became depressed that's when...well, you remember the rest of that short life. When you finally died though, your soul was in such a deep dark depressive state that it nurtured the evil within. The evil that all souls are born with. Yours grew to be a strong part of you. I don't know where I was all I remember is watching you go through all of it not knowing why I couldn't move or speak. Then...when you reborn again I was too."

"Why didn't you find me then when you were old enough?" I asked.

"Your pain turned to rage and the rage became vengeance. You were reborn vengeful. It was a woman that killed me so you hated women and you hated being one, well...a human one. Your hate cut me off of contact. Antony waited in the darkness of his own shadow to take advantage. When he did, it made it impossible for me to find you. The hell you were sent to for the things you did, I could not enter not even to reach your mind. I thought you were lost forever. You couldn't even imagine my excitement and surprise when Michael found us. He was your keeper. So I knew that if he was here on earth then you were too," he finished.

'My keeper…that means no matter where I am he's not far away. My eyes got wide and I stopped instantly. Keyoni stopped a step ahead and looked back with confused concern. I looked at him. Epiphany was written all over my face. "Michael…Oh my god!" said then rushed to saddle my camel

"What?" Keyoni pressed.

"He's alive we need to make hast. I think I know how wake him." I replied. The other's heard what I said and weren't far behind me. Keyoni was already there talking to Lee.

Keyoni came in with a thud that bounced the sand. Lee came to him worried. "Keyoni. What happened? Where are the others?" Her tone was as worrisome as the look on her face.

"They're right behind me," he informed then he put one hand on her shoulder and leaned in to whisper. "The rest of the people here don't know about Pan's vampire issue right?"

"Right," Lee whispered back.

"Good. Let's keep it that way. Come one." Lee was clueless but listened nonetheless. Keyoni had read my mind so he knew but did not want to raise Lee's hopes. He sidetracked her by having her, Able, Silus and Tyron distract the rest. Keyoni readied Michael.

I came into the caravan while Myrah, Nomed, and Hahn made sure Lee stayed clueless. Keyoni handed me a small dagger but before letting go he asked, "Are you sure about this?"

"No, but do you have a better idea?" Keyoni got the point. I made an incision on my wrist and drained it into a medium sized bottle filling it just a hair over half full. I handed the bottle to Keyoni then wiped the blood off my wrist while the wound healed. I kneeled down and held Michaels head in my lap. With my thumbs gently placed on his temples. "Go ahead," I prompted.

Keyoni knelt beside Michael, opened his jaw, and began to pour the blood in. "Ooohh he is not gonna be happy about this. It's not going down," Keyoni said.

"Well it has to. We got to get his throat to relax," I remarked

"We? I am not doin that! You do it. You should know," he stressed then Keyoni looked at me in fear from realizing what he just said. I gave him an evil glare then slightly grinned evil. I laid Michael's head down, "You know," I started as I stood up, "you and my brother really need to learn when to keep your mouth shut!" I exclaimed as I harshly shoved him out of the caravan. I turned back around to see Michael holding himself half up by his elbows, his eyes wide with surprise and confusion and fixed on the caravan curtains that Keyoni just flew out of. I gasped with glee and cupped my hands over my mouth with tears welling up in my eyes. He looked at me still trying to wake up.

"Wow. Involuntary twitch?" Michael said. I exhaled a slight giggle. I dropped to my knees and squeezed him.

"I wasn't sure it would work," I said.

"Yeah well if there comes another time when I fall into a slumber like that...don't do that again. It was kind of gross."

I smiled with my arms still around his neck. "Deal," I answered.

Meanwhile...Lee noticed Keyoni's fallout and was no longer distracted. "Keyoni!" she shouted, as she jogged toward him. "What were you doing in there? You of all pe..." Lee stopped mid-sentence and gasped very deeply when she saw Michael step out of the caravan after me. In the speed of light she engulfed herself around him. She slammed into him so hard it caused Michael to fall back into the caravan with her in his arms.

As much as we all wanted to enjoy this reunion we couldn't. We had some surprise visitors under not so happy circumstances. I could smell them two miles away and fifty feet in the air. Vampires. Something was different about these ones though. Their thoughts were screaming at me. We are choosing the right side! We come with a truce. Must hurry! No time! Danger! Lee and Keyoni almost instantly sprung up into the sky.

"No!" I snapped. Then concentrated some more. "Wait...they're not coming for a fight," I said in more calming tone. Everyone was on edge...even me...standing at attention. Ready to take on whatever could happen.

Nine of them landed down without a sound just appearing right in front of us. I took two steps forward and so did a female vampire.

Her hair was shoulder length golden ringlets that brightened her piercing red eyes. "You risked a lot to come here like this," I stated. She looked down then back up to make eye contact. My name is Domeaka. I am here with a sworn truce on behalf of...Antony." Keyoni growled so deep that I had to stop creepy chills from running up my spine. He took one step and I whipped my arm straight out in front of him. He hesitantly refrained.

"He just tried to kill me! Why all the sudden change?" I responded grudgingly.

Then I saw something I never thought I would see...Domeaka shown sincerity in her eyes, "There's something you and the other four need to know," she said softly. Suddenly, Nephora was a foot behind me saying, "Remember child. Control your fear. Open your eyes." I nodded to Domeaka. I could tell by the look he shot in my direction that Keyoni thought I lost my mind. No one trusted it but reluctantly agreed. Myrah, Elee, Ashton, Hahn, Michael, Silus, and Tyron were left in charge of the charge of the rest. Even the faithful followers were in a state of unease about it but they trusted me. Able, Keyoni, Nomed, Lee, and I left with them keeping our guard up strong.

We followed curiously for different reasons. When we arrived Antony was standing off guard, hands out two inches from his side, palms exposed. He obviously understood as much as we did about the inevitability of curiosity just as much as any other being. So he expected our arrival as well as he knew that he seeming helpless would be more convincing.

I landed closest to him and he looked up at me as if in a trance before I made myself known by merely being present. Expectedly, cause I'm not an idiot and Domeaka did say..."*The other five.*" This told me that he was not alone. When he said that, he was referring to the first seven. You do the math...so...to no surprise there Rahmeeku stood who, to the untrained eye, seemed to looking straight at us but with as much discomfort as anyone else had. His body was focused in our direction but his soul was just as locked on a ready fight as we were.

I admit that it concerned me in a different way than Keyoni or the other three. They thought of, reasonably, the threat of entrapment.

I wondered, what was so concealable that only the seven could hear or speak of it? Then it hit me that the only ones…on earth…that could know something we didn't were Rahmeeku and Antony. I peered at them and Rahmeeku step too me then with swoop of his hand in motion with his arm. "In my presence he has no power. You all are safe." He assured. Antony gave me a short innocently sorrowful look that chillingly made me realize that the situation was more serious than anyone of us knew. He had never, not once, shown any kind of…in any way shape or form…vulnerability, but I could see it and from the sound of Keyoni and Lee's thoughts, I wasn't the only one.

Able wanted to tare Antony limb from limb but restrained himself when Keyoni assuringly nodded. Nomed remained naturally neutral and leaned against the wall with no concern as Lee sat next to Keyoni while I stood and just crossed my in a way of saying with body language…Just tell me. I don't have time for unknown stress. I saw Rahmeeku Glare at the back of Antony's head as of searing something into his mind.

"Look, " Antony started then glared back at Rahmeeku while saying, "we haven't been honest with you…at all in this life."

I put my hands on my hips and said, "Oh, cause you have been in every other life."

He jerked to me and I had to put out my arm again to hold back Keyoni. "Yes, I have!" He sternly put. "Even if it was bad enough to end me, you always knew what I was up to aside from this life," Antony continued. "In this life you were born with the knowledge of good and evil. More good than evil but…with your mother's death and both of your guys' suffering combined." Rahmeeku started, but Antony interrupted, "One thing you forgot though was why you choose the good for mankind…The monster I brought back to life." Antony finished. Keyoni, Able, Lee, and yes even Nomed radiated an emotion of remembering regrettably lost knowledge. Then, like a tsunami, something hit me and I have to admit, it was suspiciously chilling. As all seeing as I was supposed to be, how was it that so much seemingly important information could be so hidden from me? Rahmeeku was not pleased with Antony's hesitance so he harshly tapped the middle of Antony's spine with the top of his staff. Antony winced.

"I thought the lie would be more motivating, and it was fun but…"—Antony whipped his head back at Rahmeeku then slowly back to me—"someone convinced me of the unavoidable fact that the truth would come out no matter what, so here it is…" Antony added then took a quick deep breath and exhaled nervously then continued, "Adrianna is not your daughter. You've never had a child,," he spoke quickly then crouched with an added whimper. My need to know more and my acceptance to not be surprised by anything kept me calm enough to ask him to continue. I put a hand on his shoulder and gave a beckoning look for him to confess. I could feel it…he was awkwardly becoming the new alliance that no one expected.

Some of the Reality

"The reason you struggle with some of your thoughts, memories, and the evil within is because they're not all yours," Antony said. I curved my eyebrows in ward but stayed quiet. He went on, "The pregnancy and the last life, spent raining terror with me...it was your twin." My eyes got wide as I gasped lightly but deep. Then I shot my head back at the others. I was furious. It wasn't about the information; it was about the ridiculous extent that I felt I had been lied to.

I wanted to explode but needed to hear the rest so, I closed my eyes and took a deep breath while slowly turning my head back around to face Antony. "Look. Everything that you were told did happen. No one lied except for me. The others didn't know about the missing details. Keyoni suspected something wasn't right but could never figure it out. Your real mother and father were equally opposite. They were the yin and yang of good and evil, so it only makes sense that they would bear children the same way. You guys were telepathically connected in every way. If you got hurt she would cry. If she suffered you were in pain. The life that ended with rape and torture really did happen to you. The afterlife journey of your dark decent was as described but what was not known was that it was your last life before this one. You guys were connected in fact that when you were reborn on earth she was to…When she died…" he paused

Then I said, "I did to." Antony gave a nod.

"The last life you thought you lived was her life. You guys were living at the same time." A chill embraced him as if remembering something that he enjoyed in a creepy way. He closed his eyes reminiscing and in a second he opened them to look back at me. "When I wasn't with her I was defiling your body. While letting you heal so that I could come back and do more, I was adding to the worlds victim scale with her. You were never turned though. This was what I wasn't telling you about the lurking evil. When she died she thought that she lost the child. It broke her. She didn't want to exist anymore. You pitied her and between the two of you figured out how to make her soul a part of yours. You guys combined. You didn't know until recently that your niece was alive. In taking her in, you took in the evil. The vampirism. Keyoni couldn't even find you in that decent. After she vanished it was easy to convince others that Adrianna was yours. That lie kept her protected and alive. They had no clue. Hell, no one knew," he finished.

I crossed my arms then started a glare. "But you did" I speculated.

Antony nodded then said, "I turned her. I will always know where your sister is. Keeping it from Keyoni was my way of making someone suffer with me. I loved her. Still do. The thought of him touching you is the same to me as touching her. I might be an awful being but I am not evil enough to be incapable of love or feeling the pain it brings."

Frustration clouded sympathy for me at this point. "You're an idiot," I said calmly then continued, "You actually thought it would be easier for me to consider killing my daughter than my niece?"

Antony shook his head twice slowly. "I wasn't telling you. I was telling her," he responded. Then it all made sense. The vampire that came alive in me was her pain and anger and the intoxication of just smelling Keyoni's blood would send any vampire into frenzy. Well… any except for Antony. I didn't know what to say or do. The frustration was overwhelming.

I threw up my hand and started to walk out. "I need to go somewhere. Nobody follow and stay out of my head!" I stated as I walked out then in an instant I teleported with no certain destination in mind.

Without warning I was yanked out of my teleportation. When I landed, there were two hybrids in front of me and one holding onto me from behind. My hands were held behind my back and this hybrid was pretty strong. One of the ones in front of me held a dart blower to his mouth then shot one right into the side of my neck. I tried to struggle free but whatever was on the tip of the dart worked well and fast I could feel myself fading out. The one holding me whispered brushing the tip of his lips on my ear, "Sh, Sh, Shhh." I began to go limp.

"Good girl," he said before I passed out.

I woke up comfortably laid on a small twin bed. I fluttered my eyes open still a little disoriented then shot up only to hit my head on the wood above me. It was a bed built into the wall like a cubby space just longer. I plopped my body back down with one hand on my forehead. "Don't worry. Everyone who's ever slept on that bed does it," a woman exclaimed. Her English accent was strong in her voice. I looked out and saw her come from behind sheer curtains that divided the room. She was a hefty woman in a peasant dress. I carefully got up from the bed and she approached me with a drink I looked at it with hesitation. "Go on. It's just water," she insisted. I took the water and sipped. "I understand that your invitation was startling but they didn't have time to reason with you. My name's Sarah." After she said that, the door opened and a big burly man walked in with a pile of wood in his arms. He had a big bushy beard and kind eyes.

"Ello," he said then went to tend to the fire.

"That's my husband, Jacob. You need to contain yourself, love. What I am about to tell will cause you panic." I wanted to throw up. Am I the only one that was getting tired of the constant surprise in this story? I sighed with a slight roll of the eyes.

"Okay. Now what?" I said handing her the empty cup.

"I'm not gonna soften my words to make it easier for you to deal with," Sarah began, "There is much talk that not even your precious hears about. A kind of truth that is logically coming into full circle and rumor has it that you can't, don't want to, or both...remember who this story truly tells of." In Sarah saying that I related the words to what Nephora said and then Sarah said, "Nephora's outside. She had just arrived." Sarah knew what I was thinking. But how? I was supposedly the only one being in existence that couldn't be taped into under any circumstances. Why now? What changed? Or...is what they're saying true? Are things not at all what I see? It seems that when you are what I am...you are surrounded by new, old and hidden truth. "I can't tell you what has been forgotten," Sarah added then Nephora walked in and Sarah continued "But she can help you with some if not all of it." Sarah got up after that and went behind the curtains to tend to her husband's hunger. Going on with their lives as if we weren't there.

Nephora sat down on a log that was carved to make a stool. I opted to stand despite her offers to get me a stool as well but she gave me a stern look and lowered voice in saying "Please. I insist." So I sat at sight of her summoning a stool without blinking or inhaling an extra bit. Then she began her story, "It's not the time to tell you why Sarah or I can read you so well. It will come. Right now you need to understand why you are really here. The memories that inspire you must be done on your own. But here is a start...You have never been the reason for war. No being remembers the exact moment of their creation or the reason for it if there is one. But your reason was not meant to be forgotten." Sarah emphasized as I listened closely. Everyone said that I would know if it was there to recognize therefore they thought they knew more because I pushed just about everything they knew and more away. I they saw what they could see then I clouded the rest. So it was a fact that no one actually lied to me. They only told me what they knew. After all...How could I see something that I made disappear? Nephora and Sarah were the only ones that said I forgot though. This was my point. The other's trusted that they knew more but also what I thought I knew. Apparently no one knew, or remembered for that matter, what I was about to find out.

Nephora explained more, "Keyoni was created by accident. A common accident but one that resulted for the first time, with a child. Purely innocent life. The good controlled the evil making him more powerful than anything," she said. I leaned forward with my elbows resting on my knees and my fingers intertwined to cup my hands for resting my chin to listen in even closer.

"How?" I asked slightly skeptical.

Nephora went on, "His mother was incubated by Satan himself. She was an angel. Given the fact that good took over his every emotion he was rebellious toward his father and despised his mother's weakness in falling from grace. Unable to understand the pain she bared thus... his birth on earth after his learning of you and your sister's existence. Between the two of you before you were even born...he knew...he knew who you each were then and who you both were going to be and in return, became understanding. He had, literally in every sense, the best of both worlds."

"He had tabs on every good and bad soul that came and went. But both of you were different. Most think that it was Satan's son who got a hold of your mother when in fact; it was one of his fallen. I guess he thought that what Lucifer could do he could do too. With different intentions. He was angry with Lucifer for convincing him to go against the gods and blamed Lucifer for his down fall so...He allowed himself to love and loved your mother hard. In turn the unexpected happen, starting his mission. They created not one but two pure life forms to protect Lucifer's one mistake and with the angel...your mother... with her help, you and your sister were raised perfectly along side with Keyoni until things went south. Lucifer found his moment to retaliate." She paused and memories of their death...the ambush...the first time I killed a man and something new...I didn't kill the man because of what he was about to do to me but my sister. After killing the man I thought he had strangled her to death while...you know, and left her there. I just kept walking in shock. Yet she tried to bare no ill will against me. It all ran through me.

Lucifer didn't want my help; he wanted me to forget what I was raised on and who else was raised with it at such a tender age his advantage was perfect. I looked at Nephora then asked, "Lucifer knew what they did, didn't he?" She stared into my eyes as if aging me to put the pieces together. "He's how the gods found out," I said.

Nephora nodded once then continued on, "Lucifer knew that as long as your parents were made human before you and your sisters four month bodies become of mind and soul, then the same rule would apply to you. Preventing the gods from making you one of their greatest defenders, and... Before you ask they did even consider it with Keyoni, before it was too late, because of whom the real father is... that Keyoni was their greatest hope. They got lucky with mostly good residing in him though. Take into consideration that the timeline you were told was wrong cause this all happened not longer than three years after the fallen had been banished." Nephora added and my eyes widened as I intensified my listening skills.

She talked on, "After your parents' murder and everything else you contacted Keyoni only eight months after she"—Nephora looked over at Sarah's silhouette and gestured who she was talking about with a nod—"started raising you." My hands dropped still cupped with my elbows rested still on my knees. I looked in the same direction wanting to run to Sarah with every sudden flash of memory I had with her, but Nephora put a hand on my both of mine instantly and said, "In time." I adjusted myself to tune back into her words and oddly familiar eyes.

"It wasn't just your parent's death that sprung you into this decision... it was that you learned Lucifer found a loop hole. This is why he sold your parents out. He figured out that he could, figuratively speaking, gain the all Seeing Eye... by drinking every ounce of Keyoni's blood. Keyoni's blood will gain him access that no being wants him to have. Everyone was just fine with the balance that was decided upon. After your parent's decent Lucifer had his minions waiting in the shadows."

"Okay." I interrupted. "So all this... every path that has been taken by Keyoni and I was made in Lucifer's direction?" I asked while standing up as if ready to pace.

"Mostly, the gods stepped when they could. But—"

She tried to answer but knowing what she was gonna say I interrupted Nephora again, "With the corruption..." I stopped mid-sentence, "What was Keyoni's first kill?" I asked.

"As I am truly hoping you are smart enough to figure out... around the same time of your parents' murders his were also killed. John had seen enough and kept the infant safe until found. No one knows who told him but he did find out. Thus inspiring him to think up the perfect being. One who could destroy or...create."

I gave her a one eye squinted look with my head cocked to the side in getting her point, while she told me more. "Anything in its path, all he needed was you. You knew just as well and felt the same so you were also willing which is when the First Seven were assembled. Everything after that...as you gathered...is what brought you here and now. What you forgot is what only you know. It's how Lucifer convinced you. It is what makes him so important throughout history, present and future."

I then looked at her in assurance of only one thing about it and emphasized, "It's why he was created." I suddenly closed my eyes and rolled my head around then looked back at her with concern.

My new open mind tapped into a new reality. "It's also why they have him and the others, right now," I said before I froze and squeezed my eyes shut in confusion then said, "It's not Antony. Why can't I see? Why don't I know who set us up?"

Nephora gently took my hand and cupped hers around it then looked at me with motherly pity in her eyes. I popped my eyes open looking back at her. "It is only logically natural for Antony to be the number one suspect but this time fittingly it is whom you would think entirely impossible to be," she said then added, "The reason you can't see him is because you believe it to be so far from possible. Sarah and I have brought you here to do an emergency memory recall. You were born just as innocent as any other human being is born. This good fight within you was taught. You need to remember that time." My eyes widened when Nephora finished.

Sarah came in through the curtains and said, "It is in those memories that you will find out why they are after Keyoni's blood and not yours. I fear we have all made a grave mistake in our assumption for over sixty thousand years and this world deserves our attention to that detail. We have already wasted enough time." Sarah carried a stool in with her while saying that then set it down to sit next to the small bed I laid in. I followed her every move with my eyes then looked into her eyes when she sat. I looked back at Nephora and she nodded once in assurance. I then got up and laid flat down closing my eyes without saying a word. For the first time some was gonna help me remember my soul's truth. Not my minds truth. If I was suppose to know everything I wanted to remember everything.

Sarah put the palm of her hand over my eyes with her pinky on one temple and her thumb on the other. She started speaking in old Latin and Nephora chimed in. They were calling upon every forgotten and remembered ounce of me to come forth and paint the picture in motion of why Keyoni is the one needing protection. Memories clear as a sunny day came swooshing through from…running in fields of lavender while playing with my sister. She had long black hair though mine was brown everything else was the same in our looks. The two of us would race to a woman whose beauty was within and out shined the rest of her. She had an average looking face but the body of a goddess and steal your heart bright green eyes that complimented her shining amber colored hair. Her hold on me was warm and comforting then, zoom…to another memory of playing with a pup in what I knew to be my room…

It went on and on quickly memories of harmless witchcraft between each other and communication that only my sister and I could know or understand. Then swoosh…to lessons on using a small crossbow and sitting patiently with her while watching my father, a handsome built man with kind blue eyes and pitch black hair, blacksmith two swords for someone our size. Next thing I knew we were side by side. Our father was teaching us how to fight with the swords. I remember lessons from different ages but not why yet until it finally came…

My memories jumped back to when my sister and I were just children of maybe twelve or thirteen and my parents had sat us down at the dinner table holding each other's hand. We looked at each other in hopes one knew what was going on, but telepathically we told each other the same thing, '*I have no idea.*' Suddenly an elderly man in Indian clothing stepped in and behind him…well, obviously was Keyoni. Who was just as ever so gorgeous. We locked eyes and I pulled my eyes away in shyness. My memory fast forwarded to my father explaining more.

"In his mother's eighth month of pregnancy she came to us in desperation to save her unborn sons future." Father began, "We were stumped and asked her to give us the evening to discuss it. The best we could come up with was to have a child of our own. For we thought a child that is made out of love would be just as strong as the one that was not. What we didn't plan on was there being two of you. We raised you both to work together and always love each other because of the outcome," he explained then looked at my sister and said, "You were born with most of my darkness."

Then my mother looked at me. "And you were born with most of my light. In harmony side by side you both can do wondrous things," she said.

"What kind of wondrous things?" My sister asked crossing her arms. "

Whatever is necessary," our father said. He gave one nod to the chief and the chief looked in Keyoni's direction.

I stood up quickly. "You're joking right?" I asked hoping they wouldn't do what I knew they were gonna do.

They both shook their heads twice. "One of the most evil beings in existence has come up with a plan of the worst kind. This will change everything and destroy most. You three are the only ones that can stop it from happening. How is up to you," Keyoni's father said, then I flashed to a memory of the next day after Keyoni and the chief had gone and we had finished lunch our parents explained that in Keyoni's creation the key to all things was hidden in his DNA but he was too young to be told that. It would have given him a bigger ego than the one he's got now. I dismissed it when Lucifer visited me for the first time. He convinced me that when I was born it became about me and my parent under estimated me but it was really him who under estimated me. He assisted in the idea of the first seven because he thought it would do nothing more than kill me.

My memories fast forwarded again. To when I realized that my sister loved Keyoni before I did but he had his eyes on me. In return it created the distance between her and me. This explained the reason for her absence during the first sevens' come about.

We still maintained a bond but she stayed away unless I was alone. At the time she was the only one that could hide her mind from me. So I did not know that the reason for her growing darker was because of Antony's romancing her. She understood that if I knew then I would physically take and keep her away from him. Especially after I knew what kind of soul was born in him when he became a vampire. I wasn't difficult to see that's not what she wanted.

In the last spill of my memories I unfortunately got no answers or clue to who may have been behind the recent betrayal or who Nephora was but there was something else. I shot my eyes open and embraced Sarah with a hug in remembering why her eyes were so familiar. She was the woman that found me bloody in her field after my parents' death, which my sister was not around to see and I hate to say this but…it was thanks to Antony's distraction. Sarah took me in, cared for me and called me her own. There's no explaining the comfort in being around someone who knew me as well as she did. There was no time for explanation of her lifespan or how she found her man. We let go of each other in taking two steps back and I looked at the both of them. "I know what we have to do." I said.

"Jacob!" Sarah called. He came in with a sword at his side and a crossbow on a hefty sack on his back. We held hands then transported back to what I hoped was still the army that I came with.

When we got there Michael, Myrah, Ashton, Hahn, and Elee were well aware of the ambush and did the best they could to keep everyone else calm while dealing with their own anxiety. I had gotten there just in time.

Myrah rushed to me. "We didn't know how, but we were gonna start looking for you," she said.

Michael came to me just after that and said, "Lee sent me a distress call with the location. She also told me that you weren't with them. She said they didn't want you. They just needed you out of the way. What's going on?" Everyone surrounded me and spoke normally but cast a spell that echoed my voice for all of them to hear.

"Lucifer used his most powerful weapon yet...deception. This was never about me. I was born to be the best form of protection for the one this has been about since the day he was born. Keyoni, they want his blood...all of it. There was hope that he would drain himself to keep me alive, but they are not willing to wait." As soon as I said that the ground began to rumble and the air dropped temperature while clouds, dark enough to blend into the night sky; closed in. The clouds swirled around causing my hair to whip my face violently. Everyone there readied for a fight but then froze. Ice encased them all. Then behind me I felt a fire so intense it could burn the sun to the ground. I turned around and stepped back. The fire disappeared to reveal a man. Tall and muscular, his eyes were golden and resembled someone eyes that I had known well. The eyes brought out the small golden strands mixed into his light brown shaved hair.

"Who are you! And what did you do to them?" I asked with aggravated concern pointing to the flesh popsicles behind me.

"I saved them from burning at the mere sight of me and I am Keyoni's one true father but I prefer to be called by name. You know me as Lucifer," he said I gasped taking one step back then I glared suspiciously at him.

"Then how could you be my grandfather?" I asked.

He became irritated and was in my face then said, "Because I am not and never have been a grandfather not you or anyone else's." His eyes seemed to be turning black as he huffed once at me.

I greatly questioned his ability to be honest so I asked, "How do I know if you're telling the truth?" He huffed and puffed more than the fire burst around him causing me to fall back on my bottom. I shuffled back then got up as fire and sand conquered the wind. I covered my face then it quickly calmed yet, I could feel a breeze pulsate like wings creating a draft. I took my arm down then looked up to see a dragon the size of Japan with golden eyes that looked like two oddly shaped stars and I'm not talking the five or six-pointed stars. His eyes were the only lights in the sky because his pitch black winged body swallowed the night sky. Then the stars reappeared and a ball of flame game down in a matter of seconds. The flames dissipated as he landed on one knee then slowly stood.

"Okay," I started, "that explains his anger issues, but it's still not reassuring." Lucifer lost his little ability to stay somewhat calm and raised his voice. "Do you think I would waste my time and risk everything I am risking to coming here to talk to you! The gods started this war. Every time they messed up I was the fall guy. I always have been. When evil becomes unmanageable for them, who do you think they send to clean up the mess! I have been a good sport up until they made it personal," he paused still huffing. I gave a judgmentally curious slight glare.

"What do you mean personal?" I wondered.

"First you need to know that your soul is a lot older than you think it is. This all started millions of years ago. When I accepted the duty to control all demented, demonic, and just plain evil souls, I was honored. It's an important job. If hell does break loose I am the only one that can put it back together. I was literally made for it. But what I didn't realize was the set up. When I figured out what they were doing I still harbored no I'll will." He gritted between his teeth. He inhaled deeply closing his eyes, exhaled then opened his eyes and looked down lightly tapping the sand like a child. That's when I decided to accept that he was at least trying to tell some of the truth because at that moment I saw the impossible...vulnerability of an innocent child in the devil himself. Even in your average man you only see that when the toughness had been softened by a woman he loved deeper than his soul could dive.

He looked back up at me like he heard what I thinking then continued with..."She was an angel. Their first. We had fallen in love before the job was even necessary. One night we were discussing the arrangement. She disagreed with the deception but I asked her to stay loyal and she did. She hid the pregnancy from the gods for as long as she could. When the gods learned of the child they ordered her to terminate the pregnancy or they would do it. And neither one of us knew why but at the same time we didn't care. It just wasn't an option for us so...your father who was wrongfully assigned to hell and became my only other ally, your mother prosecuted by the gods for lovingly a hell bound soul that needed it and I hid her the best that I could." He paused then looked down to his side trying to hold back tears. Yes… tears.

He looked back up at me with hurt, angry eyes and continued. "They found her the night she came knocking on your parent's door. She figured out that the rule of untouchable innocence applied to the unborn infant but they could still kill her after the child was born. In turn they tried to dispose of me as well so that no one would be around to care for the child in hope that it would die shortly afterward and that's when it became personal."

"But why would they want him dead?" I interrupted with hand movement.

"They feared his perfectly combined powers and with stupid reason. As conceited as the gods were, they could not handle someone created by what was beneath them, being as great or let alone greater than them. It was because of them I turned cold." Lucifer began to grit through his teeth again and begrudgingly continued.

Hanging his head again Lucifer then said, "Because of the gods and their all knowing there was no where I could hid her but I could keep the child safe. They can't touch a mystic sworn to neutrality so I had no choice but to allow a demon attack on the ship. I knew the right ones would find him. What turned me cold against them and the human race was having to sacrifice my wife and unborn child to protect them from having to take on the wrath that the human race would get the butt end of…only to turn around and see everyone and everything twist, turn and perverse what was known as equality. Before I took this job, no one was better than the other even if their riches could climb as high as Everest. The rich were actually generous then and the poor were more able to get rich. I admit I ruined that after they…like I said before…made it personal. You have every right to judge me. I am not trust worthy and I care no more…to this day, about the human race. But I will always love my son. He is a part of her and, the only good part of me that is left. Please believe me when I say that I am here to help…just this once and this one time only." Lucifer seemed to be done with explanation at that point.

I felt like I was in one of those stories where the crap never ended making you not wanna hear or read anymore of it. It was all becoming too much. "The elixir—"

"The Elixir," Lucifer interrupted impatiently then went on, "was to bring back the warrior in you with the confidence of your immortality. So that you would remember just enough. For obvious reasons I can't stay but there is someone who can help. Someone you know. If you want more answers talk to him." He finished then disappeared in a split second.

It all made sense...Keyoni had always been the one. How else do you hide the most powerful weapon in all existence? By making everyone believe it was something else. Like they say...Deception is the devil's greatest victory. I could feel the chill in the air becoming warmer and everyone unfroze. They all looked around confused and a few chatted with each other. I look straight to my left instantly sensing a well known presence. John. Who, I assumed, was the one that was going help me.

Michael came to me, "Are you okay and what the hell is going on!" he asked with extreme concern. "Look..." I started, "I promise, I will tell everyone everything but we need to move west now!" I stressed without raising my tone. Michael grit his teeth but then settled himself and moved on.

I took Lucifer's advice and asked for more answers from the right being. John informed us that Adrianna and her army had moved to an underground of their own. It was beneath the grounds of an abandoned and well hid fortress. We all gathered ourselves in a wagon and all began to discuss our route.

The decision was that it would be better to split into seven groups consisting of twenty people. Each group would go a different direction, but we would all meet up at the same place causing the enemies' watchful eye to spread out.

Execution

My mind was spinning and both sides of me wanted to explode. My mind couldn't reach Keyoni. I feared the worst as did the others. We all marched on with heavy hearts. Little did I know that they were waiting, but my sister would warn me just barely on time.

In a day and a half, we were not much closer to the destination but we were still making progress for we started to see more and more trees. The night sky was beginning to take over as the second day was coming to an end. We were treading quickly and silent. Not many words had been said for worry was weighing down our minds. I stopped suddenly. My eyelids fluttered as my eyes rolled into the back of my head. I felt an outstanding force tingle throughout my body. My veins pulsated. My muscles shuttered and my heart was pounding so hard that my chest seemed to pulsate with every beat.

More of my sister's memories whipped around. Blurry at first but then started becoming clearer and I began to realize what was happening. She was trying to come through. According to John and Michael there was a small shock wave then I fell on my back as I found myself by the oak tree my sister and I would play by. I was a little girl again. Like I had gone back in time to my first life. I had light brown long ringlets with sparkling light green eyes shaded by my thick, long and black eyelashes. I looked around. A light gust of wind made strands of my hair dance in the air. I could smell tulips and I looked upon a field of them. The soft cool grass was comforting beneath my small bare feet.

I heard a couple small footsteps and looked to the tree. Another little girl that looked like me came out from behind the tree slowly. She kept one hand on the trunk and grinned. In three quick steps I hugged her tight and she squeezed back. When we released she smiled then ran. I followed. We ran down a small and short hill side giggling, then into the field of wild tulips. I caught up and we joined hands then spun around laughing. She fell back from dizziness, and I went with her landing on top, then I rolled off of her onto my back, and we laughed hard then began to stare at the blue sky. Watching a couple bright white clouds slowly float by.

We heard a buzzing noise coming closer. A beautiful dragonfly came into view and we watched it land on a yellow tulip. The tulip swayed trying to balance the weight. My sister slowly sat up on to both knees with her back to me then carefully cupped both hands around the dragon fly. "What are you doing?" I asked sitting up.

She turned to me, "Adrianna can see you because of me. I can help that if you allow me to give you this gift," she answered. She could tell I was wondering how a dragonfly could help but my curiosity was strong. I got up on to my knees as well and held out my hands while she closed her eyes and whispered something to the dragonfly. She looked up at me and smiled. "Turn around," she said softly. I was confused but did so anyways. "I am dreadfully sorry but this is gonna hurt a little," she said and before I could give it a second thought she slapped her hands on my back. It felt like someone had dumped gunpowder on my back, made a design then lit it with a match.

Not knowing what was going on Michael freaked out at the sight of my body levitating ten feet up then dangling in the air like I had been tide to an invisible cross. John had to restrain him. I opened my eyelids to reveal my eyes to be as white as can be then jerked my head back with the look of agony on my face, unable to scream or even whisper. On my end everything went black. My sister's adult face came through then she whispered in my ear, "Trust me please. You can trust him." I awoke gasping for air when I felt my body drop into someone's arms.

I focused my eyes to see Antony's face. I jumped to my feet. "No!" I stressed with both hands out to stop Michael and others from tearing him apart. Antony had already disappeared though. I knew he was still close though. "I know that you've been trying to protect me. Adrianna can see your every move. So you made sure my hate for you ran deep enough to stay away from you." I called then in a regular tone I added, "I have forgiven the past." Antony showed himself slowly stepping out of the dark. He stood five feet from me.

"You are the only part of her love and beauty that I have left. I know it was dumb to come here, but I could feel her coming alive inside of you. I had to say sorry to her about Adrianna and beg you to accept our help," Antony said.

I squinted suspiciously. "Our help?" I questioned.

More vampires and a couple of hybrids came out of the dark and stood behind him. "How did you escape?" Michael asked.

"They still thought I was on their side. I told them I was scouting and since I have the trust of the one who even Adrianna trusts... nobody questioned me," Antony replied.

My eyes got wide. "It wasn't you that betrayed us, but you know who did," I stated.

Antony nodded and said, "It's why I didn't reveal the truth about Keyoni to you and them. He didn't want me to inspire the warrior within you any more than it was. His power far exceeds my own so I could not defy him with him in the same room."

I put everything together quickly. "Rahmeeku," I said in disbelief.

"What!" John's voice boomed. He was beyond angry and luckily for us John was the only one on earth that Rahmeeku couldn't touch.

"So much for neutrality," Michael remarked.

"Don't worry he will be reminded of his place in all this." John gritted through his teeth. John whipped his arms straight out while closing his eyes and incanting in his mind. He then brought his hands together as if ready for prayer and bowed his head still chanting with closed eyes. Suddenly he shot one hand to the sky, opened his eyes then shouted some words in an unfamiliar language.

The wind grew strong and black clouds rolled in. A bolt of lightning the size of a Birch tree trunk came from his hand and collided with a bolt from the sky sending the spell like a high speed wave of energy through the air. After that, the starry night shown through the clouds as they dissipated. I looked over to John. "Now Rahmeeku can predict nothing more about us," he said.

"That's great for future reference, but he already knows where everyone is. Your telepathy is powerful enough now that you can tell the other groups to prepare for an immediate attack," Antony informed. I did as he suggested and we all took stance as well.

I have to admit…without Keyoni being able to take full form to escape, burning all in his way, and aid us…I was nervous. But I swallowed it down quickly. If I am Keyoni's protector than I needed to fight fiercely and this time it was me who had to stay alive to save him. *Show no mercy…No mercy.* I kept telling myself. The smell of sulfur grew strong as the wind picked up. We could hear winged talons coming closer as the wind swirled more and more. The leaves from nearby trees rustled while the wind picked up speed.

As I looked toward the sky I could hear Michael whispered, "Where are they?" Just then I gasped at the sound of a sword being thrust into something behind me. I spun around quickly to see three inches of the tip of a swords blade sticking out of a demons stomach. It was pulled out and as the demon dropped to the ground I saw that it was Antony who slayed it. The demon twitched violently then in one smooth and instantaneous motion Antony plunged the sword into its neck. He looked to me and widened his eyes. Just as soon as he did so, I unsheathed my sword and flipped the blade back sliding it deep into the beast behind me as it tried to lunge for me.

Antony ducked and spun around slicing a demon upward while I swung my sword over him decapitating another. John used his gifted hand and disintegrated five of them at once.

I stupidly became distracted in seeing Michael's vampiric strength and carnage. I was proud but disturbed at the same time. With my guard down something slammed me to the ground with a loud thud causing me to drop my sword. My sword landed right by my head with the handle right in front of my forehead on the ground. I spotted it but the thing had jumped on top of me. While trying to hold it back I saw what and who it was. A vampire. One that I knew. He was from my past life that Antony shortened and horrified. Antony would let him have his way with me privately. Once every six months. Free to do as he pleased. His extensive cruelty kept me in fear as the six months turned into only a few days until he came back for more.

His name is Markis and he was grinning. He was enjoying the fact that he knew I knew him. I could feel my sister's fury boil up with mine in sharing the memories with me. Our powers combined with our fury and the temporarily forgotten, beast within came alive. Stronger than ever. My teeth grew quickly along with my eyes' oncoming bright purple glow. My skin changed to a paler color. I grasped onto his throat as the radiance of lightly glittering baby blue and light, light green colors with a calm lavender iridescence covered me from head to toe. It was part of my sister's gift to me.

Markis struggled to breath failing at every attempt to get me to let go. I put my other hand on his face and pushed as a light with the intensity of the sun in every way, came from my hand and shined on his face out lining my hand. He screeched in pain as he crawled back and I stood up while staring down at him savoring the payback I was giving. He slowly shriveled up into nothing. The Light engulfed him then went out leaving nothing but a few ashes floating in the wind.

My senses were more alive than ever. I could feel the change in the air and hear a very faint whistle as an arrow headed toward my back. I moved to the as fast as light then caught the arrow when it passed by six inches from my head. I could sense where this one was and quickly spun around, whipping my arm straight out. My hand looked like it was holding an invisible miniature crossbow with the arrow pointed directly at him. I gracefully blew on it and the arrow shot out hitting him right between the eyes.

We heard hissing and growling then we heard howling. The pause was over. Werewolves came charging out of the woods. One of them slammed into a hybrid that came with Antony. The hybrid shove the beast off of her with such force that it slammed into the trunk of a tree snapping its spinal cord in half. The werewolf died instantly. Six of the soldiers we brought in our group were werewolves and they gruesomely did their part. I picked up my sword and charged two werewolves head on. In three swift moves I came out on top. Just as soon I turned around to take on another; I had been tricked; a vampire grabbed my neck from behind and went for the main artery in my neck. I felt a tap then heard her teeth brake and crumble under pressure. She screamed backing up while holding her hand over her mouth. The werewolf ran then I plunged the sword into her stomach she hissed then I yanked it out. She bent downward still standing and still hissing then I took her head off with one clean swipe of my sword. The opposing side was no match for John and they knew it. No one attack him but he helped others defend themselves although this did not help the other groups.

The battle was bloody and the end of it was even bloodier. I yanked my sword out of a demon then looked around. The beast in me faded as I landscaped the devastation. My abilities stayed amplified but the rest went back to normal. Suddenly I noticed a burning wagon and Nivoku swooping from the sky. Something was wrong. I ran to the wagon as screams of a woman became clearer. It was Paelona. Panic struck me and I took on the beast within to protect my skin. Michael and John held Nivoku back as I pulled her out of the fire. They let go and he swooped her in his arms when I just barely got her clear of the fire. Nivoku slowly embraced her in his arms. She was burned badly. He held her sobbing. "What is she doing here? She was supposed to go with the Elves," John asked.

"She flew here and snuck into the wagon while you all rested last night. She then turned herself into a field mouse and hid but she fell asleep until it caught fire. Paelona communicated with me but did not know where she was. I found you too late." Nivoku sobbed. Michael got down on one knee in front of them and asked, "Why did she come." "She didn't get to that part," Nivoku answered then began to cry harder and kissed her forehead.

The beast within went away again and I looked down at her lifeless body with sorrowful pity. Michael stood and took two steps back. Nivoku held her tighter and one of Paelona's arms slid out. The back of her hand flopped to the ground. That's when I noticed that there was something lying in the palm of her hand. I bent down and picked up what was a ripped piece of paper with writing on it that read...

The potion was not to save you but to save him. Only true love can run through his veins. Only your...

"What does it say?" Michael asked anxiously. I knew what potion she was talking. I found a stick then drew the ingredients in the dirt.

"John." I beckoned then he came and looked down at it. "This potion; what exactly is it for? She knew. It's why she came. She made it and gave to me. I need to know." I said to John.

He grinned. "So it did survive," he remarked.

"What?" Nivoku asked confused.

"I haven't seen it since—" John began,

"Since when?" I asked slightly frustrated.

"Since the day after Keyoni's birth. Not only did your parents create twins but a powerful potion to be used only as a last resort. It binds you to him. As a matter of fact, it binds your soul to his." John stopped looking at me as if he was hoping that I would be satisfied with that answer.

But he was wrong and it showed when he cringed as I asked, "How?"

John sighed hesitating then said, "He is the only one among you that has not died but...in the event of his death..." he paused again but only for a second. "At the exact moment before he takes his last dying breath; if he drinks no less than half of the blood that bonded with the potion within you, he will live. He will become more powerful. Enough to win the war quickly, for now," he finished.

John looked over at Michael and saw the wide eyed panic on his face then looked back at me. "It is obvious that you already have the potion combined well in your DNA." I peered into his eyes then turned around to calm down enough to telepathically communicate with the other groups. I was so frustrated that I didn't want to know why he failed to tell me this sooner.

I turned back around. "I made contact. Myrah, Hahn, Elee, Ashton, Tyron, and Silus are all okay but we did lose a few. We're now down to 120 and there's been a change of plans. We're all going to meet fifty-two miles straight ahead," I informed then we all salvaged what we could. Nivoku wrapped Paelona in a blanket from the one wagon we had left and insisted on carrying her so we marched on.

The walk was hard. I struggled with knowing the pain it would cause him to lose me again but…I knew that he had to live no matter what. I wanted it. Besides, it's my job anyways. I could feel Michaels tension as well. He was conflicted with talk to me or not. After the last time he tried; I can't say that I blame him. He wanted to comfort me. Encourage me, but he was afraid of saying the wrong thing or putting the right words the wrong way.

I wasn't cold but I needed the comfort of my big brother so, I slowed down. I got close enough to stop in front of him and turn around with a distraught look. As he wrapped one arm with his cloak around me, I turned resting the side of my head on his shoulder and we walked like that for about a half of a mile. The next four miles after that; I pondered on everything and came to one, oddly acceptable, conclusion. I was bred for execution. It's why I can come back whenever the world is in peril. If they're in peril than they need Keyoni and he will need me.

During my pondering I had gotten so deep into it that when Antony gently put his hand on my shoulder, I jumped while a chill shivered up and down my spine. He held up both hands as if surrendering then said, "Whoa. It's just me."

"That's not comforting," I said.

Antony looked away grinning then nodded. "I get that," he said.

"Believe it or not I am just checking on you. This is the first life that you were born in with innocent ignorance."

"Well that explains why this is all so surprising to me," I stated.

Antony giggled lightly then went serious. "Please don't hit me when I say this but after the physical and emotional pain that I inflicted on you," he paused ready for a hit but I just grit my teeth and swallowed it down so he cautiously continued, "And all the pain you had endured before, combined with your sisters when you intertwined made you both agree that you didn't want to remember any of it. Even if it meant forgetting the good things along with the rest. I am sorry. I learned of the potion. I also knew what you and your sister could do so, I did what I did to you in hopes that it would make you both stay away from here permanently," Antony finished explaining.

It actually made sense but it did not excuse his horror and yet I knew that he did not want to be excused or forgiven. In his deranged mind; his love for my sister meant more to him than any other existing life and if I was the only way of keeping some part her alive than he was do whatever would seem to work in his mind. I knew he wasn't just apologizing to me but in a weird way my sister too. I also that he meant it because if a strong part of resided in me, it wasn't arguing with me to kill him if he betrayed me one more time.

"They're not gonna try to drain him until the next full moon and that's three days away, so I think we got time to give everyone a break while we have...a word," Antony added then we both stopped and faced each other. He grinned in noticing that I was fighting my own grin in understanding what he meant. He was offering me a chance to inflict pain on him.

As told earlier in the story, John knows and hears all so he stopped everyone then told Nivoku and Michael to grab a couple soldiers for assisting in preparing a proper burial for Paelona while Antony and I teleported to Scotland's infamous Stonehenge. We stood directly across each other at both ends of the circle the charged. We slammed into each other with a rippling boom and he dove hard into the ground about three-and-a-half feet. I land on my two feet like a baseball pitcher. Antony crawled out of his ditch and swiped blood off of his lower lip then looked at it. He spit out the rest of the blood to his left then smirked and mocked my stance. Antony stretched out one arm with his hand fisted then slowly turned his hand up ward.

He then opened his hand straight out then gave me the *come on* curl of his fingers. I didn't need to be told twice so I lunged at him. This fight wasn't just about relieving aggression. It was also about training. He was testing my knowledge and helping me learn how to work with the new skills.

After a couple of hours we sat on the grass with our backs resting against one of Stonehenge's great stones. During our break, I found out that the dragonfly was my sister's favorite. It explained why she chose it to represent her gift to me. There was an awkward pause then I asked, "I'm still waiting to find out why you have been trying to kill Keyoni if you're not one of them?"

"Like I said, I had to play the part. Hell, if I didn't let them use me they would have used someone else and that would've been all bad," Antony answered.

"Worse than it is now?" I said sarcastically with a grin that quickly disappeared when I saw that his answer was *yes*.

"They would have figured everything out a lot sooner if it wasn't for John and me." Antony added, then leaned out resting his elbows on his knees and looked down at the plush grass.

"What?" I asked after noticing that a hint of pride left him.

"A lot of the people that I have killed, I killed them to keep all of it a secret. To protect you, your sister, and him."

"Wait, what?" I interrupted while a smile stretched across my face. Antony hung his head down more and closed his eyes then sighed heavily. I gasped while cupping both hands over my mouth and stood up. Antony put his head in his hands, still leaning on his knees.

I dropped my hands to my side smiling big and bright. I wanted to giggle but I contained it then said, "You actually care about Keyoni… How? No, scratch that. Why?" Antony lifted his head to look at me as if about to answer the question then I said, "Whoa, hold on before you answer that. Who else knows?"

"Uh, no one," he said looking a little confused.

"Can I tell anyone?" I asked. Antony rolled his eyes. "I'll take that as a no. Damn. Okay I will be a good girl," I said taking a deep breath in. Then I slowly released it and looked at him with a straight face.

"He's my brother."

"Oh," I said slightly disappointed in the fact that the news was less exciting than I had anticipated then I added, "You know, that was not as surprising as I thought it would be. It actually makes sense of a lot of things. Does he know?"

"Yeah. Hell is not exactly a kid-friendly place. I left when I was eleven. I went looking for Keyoni. Our father couldn't stop talking about him. So yeah I knew about him. I was an accident. My mother was a human, whom couldn't get pregnant, but he didn't know or just probably forgot; that rule only applies to the laws of man. My mother and I both died after thirty-six hours of labor. Of course the gods sent me to my father. He had no choice."

Antony paused and looked down again then like he knew what I was thinking; Antony answered the next few questions in my mind. "I leave on good terms, so I didn't find out where Keyoni was. I didn't find him until four years later, when I found you, " he said then looked up at me.

"That's two before I met you." I said looking confused.

Antony stood up then cautiously came in close. I stepped back and he stopped putting both hands up with a grin. "It's okay." he said softly, then suddenly Antony was behind me.

He didn't touch me; he just leaned in close and whispered, "The aroma of your aura is still overwhelming sometimes." I instantly turned around, and he was gone.

"I was traveling by." Antony started. I turned back around to see him sitting down again and he continued. "I was going to take a short cut through a field when I saw a light from a lantern floating in the distant woods. Then I felt you. Naturally I was drawn so, I followed. I could almost smell the sweet life inside of the closer I got. It was a different kind of energy though. I stayed quietly out of sight and hid in the shadows. You came to a small lake and elegantly dipped one foot in. About a foot away you laid down a blanket, set down the lantern and a smaller cloth then you turned your back to the woods and slipped of your dress." Antony stopped and smiled at me mischievously.

I crossed my arms and rolled my eyes then said, "Continue."

He giggled lightly then looked back down and picked pieces of grass then went on, "I was knelt down and almost fell back. You heard a leaf crunch then covered your breasts and whipped your head back peering into the dark. You looked right at me and didn't know it. Then you started swimming. Every move you made was purely graceful. You came up taking a deep breath then went back under water and next thing I knew; my mouth was covered and a knife was to my throat. I'm sure you know who it was. We left quietly and talked. For obvious reasons he asked me to stay clear of you until he got to know me a little better. When I met you and your sister…well, you know the rest," Antony finished.

I softened my look, dropped my arms, and sat back down next to him. "Yeah, I do," I said crossing my legs then I leaned forward.

"You should know that if I'm not any better than I would not have controlled myself this long," he added.

I nodded in arrogance then could hear John coming through in my mind. "We should go. Everyone's ready. They're gonna wait to do the burial till we rendezvous with rest. It will be nightfall and the moon should be in the right place. We gonna burry the fallen together," I said. Antony nodded then got up with me and we went back.

A Simple Plan

We met up with the surviving army and held a burial ceremony. With only a day and a half left; the ceremony was sweet but it had to be quick.

Afterward Nivoku, Myrah, Michael, Elee, Hahn, Silus, Tyron, John, and I held a meeting in a wagon to discuss our plan of attack then we introduced our plan to the army.

It was simple; our last day went by and the night began its decent. The moon would reach its fullest by midnight and with only five hours left we had to execute our plan quickly so I risked the teleportation. Upon arrival, John led us as close to the rickety gates as safely possible. We hid in nearby bushes and took advantage of the shadows some trees provided. I looked over at Nivoku and gave him the go ahead nod. He instantly took the form of an asp. Nivoku balanced his slithery body up straight and hissed his tongue at me then burrowed into the ground. All we could do was wait.

It was all too easy. An asp being so common in these parts nobody was alarmed when Nivoku dug his way under the walls and came up on the other side then slithered his way into the fortress. Beasts and monsters of all kinds were there. He saw live nightmares and hideous creations that had never been seen before. Upon seeing a small fly pass by; Nivoku quickly turned into a fly also and began his search for Keyoni and the others.

The fortress almost spiraled deep underground. Nivoku could feel himself getting closer to his brother because he could sense his energy stronger and stronger. He turned down a walk way that was an arch like shape twisting and turning like a tunnel. Nivoku stopped when he came to the end of the tunnel where a silver door protected by gold strands that coiled and connected all over stood tall and strong. Each golden strand ended at the hinges and the other ends made an odd keyhole under the door knob. He landed in the keyhole and carefully crept forward. Before exiting the keyhole someone passed by so he zipped out and over the nearest corner.

Nivoku could feel Keyoni's energy swarming the room. With his buggy eyes Nivoku saw Rahmeeku and Adrianna surrounding a tall bed carved out of stone while debating about the dangers and flaws of their plan. Nivoku could see the bottom half of a man lying still on the stone bed Adrianna stood in view of seeing the rest of the man. So he swooped over to the corner adjacent to the one he was in and had to contain his sudden panic in realizing the motionless body was his brother's. Nivoku decided to listen when he saw Rahmeeku get in Adrianna's face then say in fearful frustration, "You are seriously underestimating her and him if you think it will work that way. I took this side because I believed that you were smarter than that." Then he stormed out slamming the heavy door with an angry force.

Adrianna threw a rock at the door and growled. "Stupid old man," she said then turned and leaned over Keyoni. "You just wait. She will get here just in time to watch you take your last breath," she said to him. Nivoku then flew out through the keyhole and followed

Rahmeeku to a cell were the others were being held. Lee stood up with angry eyes and put one hand each on a bar.

Rahmeeku stepped in close and said quietly, "I was regretfully wrong. Be ready." Then he disappeared. Nivoku took his human form when the coast was clear.

Lee gasped. "Nivoku. How d…," she started to ask him something when she looked down and noticed that he was naked. Her eyes got big and she spun around, thought quickly then ripped some cloth off of the bottom of her dress. Lee stuck her arm through an opening between two bars offering the cloth to Nivoku with her head turned away.

He grinned and took the cloth. "What? You've never seen something so amazing?" he asked sarcastically.

"Oh my god. You have you have your brother's ego. Look we don't have time for this. Make it into a loin cloth, diaper, something. I don't care just cover that thing up," she expressed.

Able was sitting against a wall with his arms crossed and Nomed was lying on the ground with one arm resting on his forehead. They both chuckled at her. Nivoku tied it then said, "Okay. Okay. The temptation is gone."

Lee rolled her eyes to him then gave an evil glare. "What are you doing here?" she asked impatiently.

Nivoku came in close. "Everyone's here waiting for my signal. We're coming for you guys and Keyoni," he said then turned to leave when Lee grabbed his wrist.

"Wait," she said. Nivoku looked back at her then stepped close in again. "Adrianna is going to sacrifice Keyoni's body by draining him dry and drinking his blood. She will take on a part of him and the world will be in more danger than ever." Lee added. Nivoku nodded once then turned back into the asp in her hand just to creep her out and it worked. Lee gasped dropping him and growled under her breath while glaring at Nivoku as he slithered away. After making his way outside Nivoku then turned into a crow and soared to the sky blending into the night.

I was crouched next to a tree behind a bush. I heard Nivoku land on the other side of the tree. I handed him the clothes he was wearing before he left and while he got dressed I asked, "So what are we looking at?" "There's twenty at the front gate, twenty at the back, twenty at the west gate, ten at the east gate and over four hundred more inside the fortress," Nivoku answered then crawled around to my side and crouched next to me.

"Sounds like fun," Antony said sinisterly. He was suddenly on one knee close behind us. We turned our heads to look back at him and shuttered a little not expecting him to be so close. It caused Nivoku to stumble back on his bottom. I sighed and set my eyes back on my target of interest.

"You gotta stop doin that." I said.

Antony chuckled lightly.

We made our way back to where the army was posted out of sight. Myrah approached me first. "Well?" she asked as Michael came and stood next to her.

"There's about five hundred of the worst creatures out there, some of which we know nothing about. We need to draw them out the front while I and ten others go in through the east gate. It will be lightly guarded and they would expect us to try the back." "Sounds like you need a distraction." Silus said stepping forward. "It just so happens that my brother and I possess a certain set of skills that we picked up along our many journeys," he added then stepped back and began to move his hands like reiki. Reiki is an ancient Chinese ritual to enhance your chakra a.k.a. aura, which is the energy that radiates from your soul.

Suddenly the ground was lightly vibrating. The earth beneath his feet started to rise and formed three steps then leveled back down. Silus stepped aside and Tyron came forward, did some reiki then held his hand straight out, snapped his fingers and opened his hand to reveal a small flame dancing on his palm.

Everyone looked at them wide eyed. "Why didn't you tell us that you could do that?" Michael asked.

"No one asked and we haven't needed to use it," Tyron answered.

I turned to Nivoku and asked, "Can any of the shape shifters here mimic a dragon's roar?"

"Yeah. Why?" Nivoku looked confused.

But Michael caught on quickly and said, "We're gonna need one that can roar like a dragon and shift into something big enough to fly and carry Tyron." Myrah and Hahn looked at each other confused then to me. "Pan, why don't you just ask Elee?" Hahn asked pointing to her sitting on the ground sharpening her dagger. I looked over at her then back at Hahn in question.

Hahn grinned then chuckled. "Able was right. You need to be more in touch with those senses of yours. Elee's a hybrid because her mother was a vampire and her father was shifter." Elee got up and gracefully joined the group.

"I heard my name," she said softly. I looked at her with surprise then asked, "Can you roar like dragon?"

"I can do better than that," she said smiling big then she stepped back and bolted into the sky. Suddenly a black dragon blanketed the sky, and let out an earth trembling roar. Wind picked up from the wing and everyone was in awe as the wind whipped around us.

"Oh I like her," Antony said smiling.

We could hear some commotion coming from the fortress. "Well, we got their attention." Myrah said. Elee landed back down with a light thud and nodded at Tyron. Everyone looked at me. I had to think quickly.

"Uh…Okay, Tyron get on her back and throw the biggest spits of fire that you can summon. We need them to think its Keyoni. Myrah and Michael. I need you guys to hold things down here with Silus, Tyron and Elee. John…wait, where's John?" I paused noticing that John was nowhere to be found. Little did I know that he was way ahead of me on a similar plan of his own with a different target.

When Nivoku got back from the inside and gave his estimate of soldiers, John took off and found his own way in. He is not a force to be reckoned with so eliminating guards at the west gate caused some of the guards from the east gate to come and aid in the fight. Just as I began to wonder; I got a strong message in my mind from John. "Hurry you only have a ten-minute window."

I looked at Hahn, Nivoku, and Antony then said, "You three each gather two soldiers to come with us like, now."

Michael then gently grabbed my wrist. "Pan, wait," he insisted. "Be careful." Michael said looking at me with worry. I smiled compassionately then gave him a quick hug and ran off. I quickly snuck about the bushes then sprinted toward the east gates when I got close enough with the others not far behind.

John kept the fight quick and quiet enough to not draw attention from the front or back defenses. Just as soon as I got to the gate, John got it open enough for us to slip right through with stealth. John closed the gate softly and we stayed hidden by the big doors. Nivoku then began to lead us to the main entrance of the fortress but there were a few road blocks up ahead.

The first one was a vampire. It came at Nivoku with a spear. Nivoku leaned to the side, grabbed the neck of the spear with both hands stopping the vampire instantly. It hissed at him showing its sharp fangs. Nivoku pushed the spear up with such force that it hit the vampires face and nock it back causing it to let go of the spear. Nivoku then swung it around and shot it right between the vampire's eyes flawlessly. Just as Nivoku let go of the spear a hybrid raced past Nivoku headed straight for me.

Hahn was in front of him in a heartbeat with his hand on the beast's neck. Hahn just as soon slammed him on his back. They growled at each other then Hahn stood up fast ripping out the hybrids voice box and breathing heavily as he watched it joke on its own blood. Our attention was drawn ahead with more coming. John rushed us through the main entrance and closed us in then instantly turned into a black cloud that devoured the creature's coming to attack. After wards he dissipated in the air and searched for his victim of interest.

Inside we looked around on guard. I went to step forward and Nivoku stopped me with one arm straight out in front of me. "Shhh. Something's not right." He whispered. I tapped more into my senses and he was right. It was completely quiet not one enemy in sight and we knew that they weren't all at the front gate. I knew it was trapped and I could feel it coming. Now was the time I needed to think about how to separate myself from them.

I brought my beast within to life again. Then I took one step, "Oh, Adrianna." I taunted. "Must we play these childish games?" I asked rhetorically then I taunted some more, "Your mother says hi… and she's very disappointed in you." I got close to the balcony and looked up and down the spiral hallway then hopped up on the edge of it and stood up. I balanced myself turning around to face the others. I winked at Antony and he knew what I was about to do.

He leapt forward with panic in his eyes and said, "No." holding out his hand as I closed my eyes, spread my arms out and fell back.

As I began my decent, John was taking care of his own business. Rahmeeku was in his own room of elegance frantically packing his belongings when he felt John coming. Rahmeeku grabbed and tightly held on to his staff, which was never too far away. He whipped around with the staff and saw John standing there in his original creepy form then said, "I was corrupted. I know now that I was wrong."

This was not good enough for John so he replied, "I allowed these gifts because I trusted everyone of you to obey the laws of balance and now, after so long you have decided to forsake all that. You best of all should understand my anger in this. You will reap the consequences that you feared coming."

In saying that John readied his staff as if it was a spear and Rahmeeku stood at a fighting stance. They ran at each other and collided like a tidal wave hitting the shore just as I leaned into my fate backward.

As I fell, winged demons began to swarm with each level that I fell beyond. One demon had grabbed hold of me. I unsheathed my sword then flipped it around just in time to land on one knee on top of it. The landing caused my sword to run right through him. I yanked it out and began slicing and dicing the demons that flew at me until one point in the situation that I ran my sword straight through a demon's chest. Another demon came at me from behind and held onto the sword with my right hand while I put my left hand to a demon's face who was trying to be sneaky. The sneaky demon dissipated and I suddenly got an idea that I had to take charge of before the ability faded.

With stealth swiftness; I twisted the sword that was still stuck in the other demon then yanked it upward, splitting him in half. I spun the sword twice with that same hand then grasped it with both hands and slammed the sharp ended handle into the ground quickly turning my head away.

A light more intense than the sun burst throat the tip of the sword and engulfed the hoard of demons with white and blue fire that incinerated them all in three pulses. As the ashes fell my sisters voice kicked in telling me that Adrianna had just ran down the hallway directly to my right. So I followed in pursuit with a hoard of demons behind me. I knew that she would try to kill Keyoni to keep me from saving him. I had to convince her of something else. I knew that I had to have a good story ready when I caught up.

*****

Meanwhile, Rahmeeku's body dented the ground then bounced. Causing him to land on his back and came down in the same fighting stance. "You would not have been given this gift without me and yet you betrayed the sacred laws that we both vowed to bleed for. Well, now I will take blood that you offered in your vow," John said. Rahmeeku said nothing. Only smirked then pointed the tip of his spear in John's direction and blasted him four feet away.

Rahmeeku sadly underestimated John. John didn't need to get up. All he had to do was lift his head to see his target and point his staff in that same direction. John's spear sent out such a force that it sent Rahmeeku through the three feet of a cinder block wall and landed him in the next room with a five foot slide on the dirt floor. Rahmeeku slowly got up then said, "I know that I was wrong but I can't' take back what I did."

"I won't let you run from the consequences!" John shouted then they charged each other again. John slammed back through a wall and Rahmeeku was stunned by hitting the floor thunderously.

It shook the earth so much that Adrianna stopped to cautiously look over her surroundings. I stopped also. She spun around with a sword ready to take me on. I put out one hand saying, "Whoa! Hold on. You have already won." I said. Adrianna began to relax the sword and slowly took one step closer. She raised the sword again in warning. I halted and put both hands up this time. "But it won't work with his blood alone." I added. Adrianna glared suspiciously but the glare went away to reveal that her interest had been sparked. She relaxed her shoulders then lowered the sword just four inches downward.

"There's more?" she asked.

I lowered my hands to my sides then nodded twice and said, "Yes. The reason why we come as a pair is because our blood combined is the ultimate power."

"And you're just offering that? Why?" she asked with that accusing glare again. I played off the look of desperation.

"Like I said I cannot win this one and if I'm going to die...I want to die with him." I said softly. Adrianna bought it and a glimpse of pity came from her eyes.

"Okay..." she said then paused and scaled me then said, "Slowly release your sword and slide it to my feet then put your hands behind your back and slowly turn around." I did as she asked then with her mind, Adrianna made my belt fasten my hands tightly together. Suddenly she was in front of me sword still pointed strong and said, "Now turn around and walk fast. We're kind of running out of time." I rolled my eyes at her barking orders as I turned around and began my walk.

During that time Antony, Silus, Tyron, and Michael fought on while making their way down the spiral hallway. Nivoku hid in the shadows as a fly on the wall waiting for the right time. Antony's beast within was comparable to that of a demon and being a part of my sister; I would see a lot of what he was seeing which made it hard to focus for a minute. His fighting was purely brutal yet every move was artistically played. My sister played an important role in helping my mind gain the strength to take control of these images. Silus and Tyron fought like conjoined twins but it was beautifully orchestrated and Michael's fighting was total rage. I think he wanted Adrianna more than I did. Little did he know that I was gonna give him the chance to be able to exact his revenge by his own hand very shortly.

Adrianna brought me into a room where we stopped to face an Iron Maiden open for visitors. "Keyoni was supposed to be in here. I had this one specially made. See," Adrianna said and pointed down to the floor of it then she continued, "It's a funnel. It feeds the blood down into another bigger funnel. The tip of the bigger funnel is as fine pointed as a sewing needle with a tiny hole to allow the blood to evenly flow out. It dips down into the room below stuck carefully into the veins of Keyoni's right arm. It was suppose to be me on that table down there. Now, if you would be so kind as to step into my box." Adrianna gestured toward the maiden of death. I took a deep breath and closed my eyes then exhaled. My eyes opened and I stepped into my mortal fate.

Before her minion fastened the spikes inside me; I sent a powerful good-bye to everyone but Keyoni. Didn't want him to wake up yet. Antony was hit hard. My sister came through with me. We both said good-bye calmly but losing her again was his last straw. Sorrow, panic, and blind fury rushed through him and yet he was not alone. Michael had taken on a transformation that he could not keep secret any longer. He was fierce. Like no other I had ever seen. Lee's blood somehow bonded with the vampire's venom and Michael's blood.

He became something eight-feet tall with eyes such a light blue that you could barely see them around the pupil. His face was almost that of a gargoyle with a human nose. Michael's fingers turned into eight inch long claws attached to human like palms. His muscles grew, his chest hardened while black and white feathered wings expanded out ten-feet long. With Michael and Antony combined they blazed through the enemy. Braking bones, tarring limbs and slashing faces open. They moved like an inferno. Tyron and Silus held off attacks from the back suddenly moving like tornados. Lee broke down crying and Nomed was anxious then, Able became angry. He took on his werewolf form and bent the bars open howling loud. Lee stood up looking at him with amazement then they all ran out. Trying just as hard to get to Adrianna. Even Myrah and rest of the army began fighting harder, more aggressive. Myrah was always able to take down three at a time, but now she moved up to six. Every execution was swift and effective. The army had begun to advance forward. They had no idea that most of my blood had already descended.

As everyone fought with their own uniquely brutal art; advancing more and more; my blood made its way further down the bigger funnel then began to bond with Keyoni's. Adrianna was waiting at his side to sink her teeth in. Her teeth grew the more she smelled my blood flowing through his. Our cells danced together sending a charge straight to his soul then suddenly…memories of mine along with the sweet smell of lavender in my hair and the sound of my voice began to awaken him. Keyoni realized whose blood it was and an angry sleeping giant had opened his furious eyes.

Adrianna was stunned and took two stumbling steps back with a gasp. Keyoni's body doubled in size. He got his feet quickly yanking the pierce arm so viciously that the funnel shattered half way up. His breathing became more ferocious and quickened at the site of my blood dripping from what remained of the funnel. His head shot over at Adrianna with a look full of so much vengeful evil that I dare say it bared a striking resemblance to his father. Lucifer felt it too, for it was the first time his son spoke to him in centuries.

Adrianna was petrified. Her breathing was shutter and her heart was shaken then she began to quiver. In a split second Keyoni had her on the ground with one hand on her throat. His other hand was balled into a tight pulsated fist raised backed and ready to smash while digging one knee into her lower abdomen. Michael, Antony and the others came bursting through the door. Keyoni shot his head back in their direction and them all stopped dead in their tracks out of pure amazement. The look in his eyes sent chills up and down their spines. The distraction barely loosened his grip.

"I…will…not…apologize." Adrianna managed to choke out. Keyoni leaned in then, from what I was told, it was indescribable evil that made his eyes wild and his sharp toothed grin.

"I don't want you to apologize…," he said then smiled wide and said "I want you to pay for your sins but…not by my hand." Keyoni then looked back at Michael again and smiled, "There's someone here who has been dying to meet you."

Keyoni stood up quickly and backed off. Adrianna coughed and gasped for air while rolling to her side. She then slowly got up onto her hands and knees. Adrianna forced herself to get up and face Michael. The look on her face seemed pitiful, but I'm sure that she was more in shock that her brilliant plan didn't work. Michael walked up to her quickly with aggravation in his eyes and yet a calm tone then said,

"Keyoni let go to keep himself from tearing you apart. Limb by limb. I'm only going to give you what you gave me." Michael grabbed and squeezed the back of Adrianna's neck then yanked her forward as the dagger in his hand dug into her stomach. She screamed loud then dropped.

Suddenly, they all heard more hoards coming their way. Keyoni huffed once instantly transforming some more. His wings stretch out six feet on each side and his muscle mass grew along with getting taller. Everyone made way for him and he darted out in a roaring fury. Tears formed in Keyoni's eyes as he slashed and burned his way to me. He knew it was too late.

Five guards in the room with me, stood ready to fight upon hearing the commotion on the other side of the door. The heard screeching and growling that rumbled the walls. Suddenly a dead silence fell and the guards grew nervous looking at each other with unsure eyes then… the door and some of the wall behind it, slowly puffed out toward them like a bubble fighting its way through. The guards began backing up a little less willing to fight as the doorway was glowing orange red and the wall around it began to crack. With an earth quaking explosion the guards and doorway were incinerated. The iron maiden fell on its side and slid across the room then landed on its back.

Keyoni stepped over the rubble that was left of the wall and looked around to ensure that there was no one else left alive in the room. His eyes were black and his monstrous look was terrifying, but when he saw the iron maiden on the other side of the room, he went back to his lustrous self in sorrowful tears. In the speed of light he was by the medieval maiden of death. He looked over it as his lungs quivered with each breathe. Keyoni then breathed in deeply and flung the door off in one tug. The door hit a wall so hard that it shattered. He said it was like dry ice enveloped his lungs and a shaky gasp hit him then he dropped to his knees. Tears flooded his eyes. Keyoni cried silently as he slowly lifted my limp lifeless body and held me close rocking.

Lee, Michael, Able, Nomed, Antony, John, and the others stepped in the room cautiously and quiet. There was nothing any of them could've said anyways. Keyoni was past words or negotiation at that point. His eyes popped open glowing red. There is no way to describe the instantaneous change in him. From grief stricken to the rage he felt at that moment. Keyoni did not turn and look at them. He only said, "I have to end this, John. Get them out of here." John nodded then the dirt swirled around them as they all watched Keyoni slowly stand while looking at my blank face. They all wanted to protest. Stay and fight to the death, but I sacrificed my life to save theirs so getting killed would have only dishonored that. They left with heavy hearts and Lee held Michael as he laid his head on her shoulder trying to not cry.

Keyoni didn't blink. He just kissed my lips then, feeling more inspired from the touch my cold lifeless lips, he huffed and puffed heavily. Like a volcano that gives warning of its eruption. His teeth grew painfully but his did not flinch. His soft silky skin became rough and scaly while his wings expanded.

Keyoni knew now what he was. My blood showed him everything. He finally knew what he was meant for and he was gonna give it his all. When someone loves another as he does me; that someone could scarcely begin to imagine the pain of losing that loved one more than once. Keyoni had enough and this time he himself would ensure my souls safe return. With the combination of my blood and his; he gained new power that evolved the abilities he already had.

He closed his eyes and whispered an ancient spell in my ear. A spell that I didn't know. His father answered his call by telepathically sending him the knowledge of this spell. Its sole purpose is to keep my soul in a dormant peaceful rest inside my body until he awakened me. If he couldn't wake, he entrusted only two others. When it was said and done, Keyoni began the transformation.

He huffed and puffed. His cheek bone's cracked and reformed while his skin was turning an iridescent black. Scales began to form while his eyes clouded over in a glowing red. He was growing more massive than ever before. His new intense power had permanently become greater. The pain from Keyoni's titanic change amplified his rage. He dropped to his knees and laid me down then laid one hand on me. Dirt swirled around us then his hell fire spit out and danced with it. The dirt melted to liquid and began encasing my body then hardened into grey marble. Every detail of me showed except for the numerous holes in my body. Keyoni shed one last tear then continued his transformation.

He grew so big that he could level a football field. The earth shook, and he sent a blazing inferno throughout the underground that opened the earth above. The enemy fell hard and fast with not even an ash left of them. Keyoni then pointed his head up and pushed through the earth like a giant drill. The earth explosively released him. He spread his wings out and in a perfect circle, he roared with blue fire extinguishing all life within a quarter mile radius. Keyoni then dove into the ground, picked me up still marble incased and burst out of the ground again disappearing into the night, taking the chaos with him. The starry sky became clear and the moons beam shown bright through the dissipating smoke. When it all settled; it seemed as though the dessert had claimed what was once there.

Keyoni hid me well, waiting for the danger to return. Whenever evil reared its ugly head he vowed to be there so that I wouldn't have to. Unfortunately, nothing lasts forever. In centuries to come, one day I will wake.

CPSIA information can be obtained at www.ICGtesting.com
Printed in the USA
BVOW03*1755300614

357642BV00002B/5/P

9 781628 387179